THREAT of
Darkness

LAUREN
DANE

ELLORA'S CAVE
ROMANTICA®
www.EllorasCave.com

An Ellora's Cave Publication

www.ellorascave.com

Threat of Darkness

ISBN 9781419965531
ALL RIGHTS RESERVED.
Threat of Darkness Copyright © 2007 Lauren Dane
Edited by Ann Leveille.
Cover art by Syneca.

Electronic book publication July 2007
Trade paperback publication 2012

THREAT OF DARKNESS

ဆ

Dedication

ജ

For Ray, who is all that and then some. God help me, I can't get enough. XOXOXO

Ann – the editor who's taught me a heck of a lot about writing – thank you.

Assorted beta readers and critters – thanks for all your hard work.

Author's Note

ജ

Threat of Darkness is set in the same universe that the Witches Knot books are. It's not part of the series and is a standalone story. But you'll find some familiar faces here, and meet some new ones.

Chapter One

ഗ

Mei wiped the sweat from her brow and dusted her hands on the front of her pants. Leaning over, she grabbed the darkling by the cuffs at the small of his back and hauled him to his feet. The muscles in her arms flexed with her exertion to keep the thing still.

He sniveled and growled but with the magical cuffs on his wrists, he wasn't able to use his dark powers against her. Truth was, she'd had it to hell and back with scum like lesser demons and her hatred was what had kept her victorious over them for the last several thousand years.

"Brimstone. I hate brimstone." She wrinkled her nose in distaste and sifted them both to the Donovan's antechamber.

"Ah, lovely Mei." Carl Donovan, a man of indeterminate age despite the appearance of a fortyish college professor, smiled at her as he approached. "Successful as always, I see. This is the lesser we sent you after last week? Quick work."

She handed him the paperwork that gave her permission from the council to hunt and capture the darkling she'd brought back. "It's him. I caught up with him in Boston.. Had to chase his stinky ass back to the eighth level. There were three bodies in his squat. Card is there cleaning up."

The Donovan, as most referred to him, looked over the paperwork, burned his signature into it, and with a flick of his wrist the darkling and the papers disappeared.

Mei conjured herself clean clothes and felt much better. Until the Donovan spoke again.

"Darling girl, I have an assignment for you." He indicated that she sit on one of his couches with the tip of his jaw.

She did of course. One didn't do anything else when a god gave an order, even disguised as a request. The room was beautiful and classic, dark oak furniture, sumptuous fabrics in deep color. A series of desks and small seating areas seemed to flow through the space. Mei had never been anywhere outside it and he'd always diverted her when she asked what lay beyond the frosted glass windows behind the big desk.

"Of course. I'm at your service."

The Donovan simply raised one eyebrow slightly and sat across from her, crossing one leg over the other. "We've got a problem. A big one of the *oh no, if you don't stop this the world will end* variety."

"How very Buffy the Vampire Slayer."

He chuckled. "Yes. Nonetheless, you'll have to go a bit farther afield for this one."

"I was just in the eighth circle of hell. What's farther afield than that?"

"Tir na nOg."

She exhaled sharply. Only the thousand years of discipline that kept her alive as a prisoner in a darkling hellhole kept her from jumping up.

"I know you are averse to any dealing with the Fae but it can't be helped. This problem needs a solution and you're it."

"I'm it? Come on, Donovan! I'm not the only warrior in your service. There are many who are much stronger than I am. More magically talented. Why not them?"

"They aren't you." He said it like it made sense.

A sound much like a growl trickled from her lips. "You know how I feel about them."

"I do. And I know why. However, the time has come to tell you that you don't know the whole truth. The truth is more complicated than that."

She threw her hands up in the air. "Oh save me from complicated! Complicated is what you god types use when you fuck with the rest of us like puppets."

"That may be so, but you don't know the whole of it."

"Because my mother wouldn't tell it to me. I went back. After I managed to escape you know I went back to Tir na nOg. My mother had a lackey tell me that my father had been killed along with my brothers and that my title and property had been taken from me. I asked for the fucking truth and they exiled me. So pardon me if I'm a little hesitant to go back there and help them out when they fucked me over so royally."

Donovan sat, fingers steepled in front of his chin, pensive. "Mei, have I ever done anything to harm you?"

"No. Of course not. Without you I'd still be in Carthau."

"I am asking you to trust me on this. It *is* complicated. But things are different now and I believe the truth you seek is easier given now for a whole host of reasons. This is important. So important I can't stress it enough."

She closed her eyes for long moments. "Okay, Donovan. Because you ask I will go."

"Thank you, Mei. I'll come with you. Freya will meet us there."

"Freya's in on this too? Okay, so it is *fate of the known universes* important."

He stood and shook his head, amused. "I'm so glad it's Freya's name that makes you snap to attention and not mine. Now you need a different outfit." With one of his dramatic wrist flicks she was transformed.

Transformed into Mei NiaAine, direct descendant to the line of queens. Her golden-blonde hair was swept up, wrapped in silver cording as it cascaded down her back in long strands. Her jeans and boots had been traded for a gown in midnight blue with the same silver cording at the waist, pushing her breasts up and her cleavage out the wide keyhole neckline. It was backless and floor-length with side slits to the waist. A band circled her upper arm on each side, bearing her familial sigil, three concentric circles.

"I..." She blinked back tears and tried to swallow the emotion as she caught her reflection in the mirror across the room. "I've been forbidden to wear these symbols. I haven't worn my familial colors in over two thousand years."

"They're yours to wear again and don't ask any more questions because I can't answer them. Not right now. I make you my promise to tell you all I can when I can. Even I have to obey some rules, darling. Now, head up, you'll be the queen someday. We're off."

"To see the wizard," Mei mumbled and she heard the whisper of his laughter as they sifted into her mother's antechamber.

It was just as Mei remembered. The beauty of the space, of her memories of growing up there at her mother's right hand. Of the joy of discovery of her powers, of wonderful moments with her family and friends. Of finding real love.

Then the pain. The pain of being told Nessa was her father and realizing a man she'd always liked and respected was her brother! Wanting so much to tell him so but having to keep it quiet because Nessa didn't know and neither did Conchobar or Finn. So she'd instead become close friends with Con and watched her father from afar, aching to know him. And because of her friendship with Con she'd fallen for Jayce. Pain and loss sliced through her heart as she remembered his laugh, the way his hands had felt on her body. His voice as he'd called her name when they'd been captured by the Dark Fae. And when she'd come back, broken and needing comfort most, the Fae had exiled her. First she'd lost Jayce and then she'd lost her father and brothers without having had the opportunity to tell them who she was. And then she'd lost her very identity. For thousands of years she'd been a woman without a country.

Rage cut through her feelings of loss as she looked around the marbled room. The floors gleamed midnight black and the walls shone in alabaster. The antechamber was easily three stories open to glass ceilings, tall columns braced the room, gave it a sturdy feeling even as it felt graceful and beautiful.

"Mei, it's so good to see you again."

Mei turned to face Freya as the goddess walked to her and enfolded her into a hug. "Freya, merry meet! You look absolutely stunning as always."

And she did. Feathers hung in the white-blonde hair that streamed past her waist. Eyes of an otherworldly blue looked Mei over with intelligence and humor. She was long and lithe and absolutely oozed sensuality and grace. She wasn't beautiful. It was more than that. Freya was the goddess of fertility and sex, of magic. She was the personification of those things and it never ceased to take Mei's breath away to be in her orbit.

"Mei, we're going in now. I've asked for a private audience so it'll just be your mother, her secretary and three of her Favored guards. She doesn't know you'll be with me. There are things you don't know. Things she doesn't know. But...I'm asking you to trust me. Can you please do that? Hold on for a bit and it'll become more clear."

Mei inclined her head. "Of course."

Freya taking one of her hands, the Donovan taking the other, the trio walked through the twelve-foot-high doors.

Aine, who'd been merrily chatting with her secretary, turned around, smiling as she saw Freya and the Donovan, and then stopped, eyes widening and mouth dropping open in shock when she saw Mei.

"No!" Aine's hand went to her throat. "It can't be! What cruel trick is this?" Her rage heated the room, made the flesh on Mei's arms itch.

Mei watched her mother through narrowed eyes until the flash of red hair drew her attention. Slowly she turned to see Jayce. Just as he saw her. She nearly sank to her knees. Would

11

have done had Freya and the Donovan not been holding her up.

"Mei?" Jayce's voice was a tortured whisper.

Confusion made it difficult to form words. "They said you were dead! They said you died the first year at Carthau!" Had he been a part of their plan to exile her?

Aine stood, her power shimmering around her, the room growing hot with it. Fury shot from her eyes. "Tell me the meaning of this evil trick immediately! How dare you come to my court with this trickery!"

"This is your daughter, Aine." Freya's voice was soft but it rang clear through the room, cutting through the chaos and silencing everyone.

"My daughter died over three thousand years ago on the battlefield in Sareem. My sister saw the body herself."

"Your sister knew Mei was taken prisoner at Sareem. She had a terrible wound. They took her to Carthau." The Donovan watched Aine through compassionate eyes.

Mei shook. Her world crumbled around her and she couldn't even process what she'd been hearing.

"No! Why would Eire do such a thing? I don't believe you. This is a trick."

"What do we have to gain from such a trick?"

Mei pulled her hands loose and stood forward. "Trick? Wouldn't that be an easy way to get around your treachery, Mother? I wish to the gods it had been a trick. A thousand years I rotted in that place. Beaten and worse. Starved of my magic. Told my lover was dead. When the Donovan found me I was… Well, I don't want to think about what I was. But I dragged myself back here and you refused to see me. Had your seneschal tell me about my father and brothers' deaths. Due to the shame I'd caused you my title and lands were stripped from me and I was exiled. What trick are you playing to stand there as if *you* were the one wronged? Has Jayce been a part of this plan from the start?"

Aine shook her head, mouth opening and closing but no words coming. "You can't be my child," she managed to whisper.

"There've been many days in the last three thousand years I've wished just that." Mei turned and pulled her hair away from the mark on her shoulder. The three circles that marked her as a member of the royal family glowed with the magic of Tir na nOg..

A sound of anguish so deep, so ragged that it tore at Mei's gut sounded, echoing through the room. Turning, she saw Jayce, tears streaming down his face, walking toward her.

"Mei, they said you were dead."

She heard the pain in his voice, the depth of loss and longing, and all she could do was look at him, at the features she'd adored so much. Still did.

Still, she wasn't sure she could trust his tears. When he pulled her into his arms a sob wanted to break from her but she held it in. He held her tight but she didn't return the embrace. Didn't know if she could. And it wasn't so simple anymore.

"Why?" Aine's voice was close and Mei looked up to see her mother staggering toward them, two of her guards flanking her. "Why would anyone do this? I buried my child millennia ago. Could it be? Oh my baby."

"It's her. She has the mark. I would not lie to you, Aine," the Donovan assured her.

"Who told you? Who sent you away?" Aine demanded of Mei.

Mei pushed herself away from Jayce but he stayed close to her. "Like you didn't know. But I'll keep playing. Brian, the seneschal. I came back and he met me at the doors to my suite. He told me Nessa was dead, that Jayce had died in the first year at Carthau and Con and Finn were dead too. He said I'd shamed you by letting myself be taken prisoner and that I'd been stripped of lands, title and property and exiled. He had an order with your signature on it. Aunt Eire came out and sent me away. I've not been able to sift back here until today."

Aine's face threatened to crumple. "I...I would never do that to you. How could you believe that? Mei, I'm your mother, I love you. I've grieved every day since they told me you'd been killed."

"Your signature was on the paper! The spell that exiled me was very powerful. Certainly not something many Fae could manage. Your own man told me you'd exiled me and Aunt Eire backed him up. What else could I believe? And no one came for me in Carthau." Her hands curled into tight fists. She still had nightmares that even Card couldn't stave off. "I waited. Goddess I waited. A thousand years I was there!"

Aine pushed Jayce out of the way and looked into Mei's face, cupped her cheek. Mei clenched her jaw but Aine wouldn't let her move away. "My darling girl, I love you. I've loved you since the moment I knew you existed within me. One reckless afternoon, oh I was stupid! But you came from that and I'd never trade it away. I didn't know. I didn't know. I grieved, I wanted to die when they told me you were dead on that battlefield. Your aunt...I don't... We'll get to the bottom of this, I swear to you. But now you're back. My child is back. You must believe me, I would have moved heaven and earth to get you out of that hellhole if I'd known you were alive!"

Aine waited, tears shimmering in her eyes as she took in Mei's face. "Please, please believe me. Let me be your mother. Let us find the answers we need." She threw her arms around Mei and the two women hugged as each one wept. Mei didn't know what to think but it felt so good to be with her mother again.

In the background Mei heard Jayce's voice harden. "Send for Eire at once. Go in person, Cullen. Do not tell her of this and bring her in the back through her majesty's personal rooms."

He stepped forward. "Majesty, we need to get to the bottom of this. Let's have Mei stand back so she can't be seen when Eire enters the room."

"How could my sister do this?" Aine stood back and looked between Mei and Jayce, confusion and pain clear on her face.

"Pull yourself together, Aine! She wants the throne, has done for a very long time and you've remained blind as she's smiled while she's lied to you." The Donovan stepped forward. "I've tried to tell you this, I know I'm not the only one." His voice was a whip.

"Don't think I've forgotten that you've never told me of Mei's existence in all these years, Carl. There will be a reckoning to pay." Aine narrowed her eyes at him and stood back, visibly putting herself back together. Placing the mantle of her leadership on like a cloak. "What do you know, Carl? Obviously Dark Fae are involved. But not Bron. He's dead."

"Eire's in collusion with the Dark Fae and has been from day one. That's obvious to us. The council has suspected for a long while that not only has Eire been with them since she sent Mei away but that she may have had something to do with the ambush at Sareem."

Mei spun. "What? You never told me this! How could you keep this from me, Donovan? My own aunt is the reason I spent all those years in Carthau? You knew and let her live?"

"I'm sorry, Mei. Yes, I've known and no, I didn't tell you. I was not allowed to tell you. I wanted to, I argued for it for millennia. But I was not allowed to reveal it until today."

"Why today?" Aine demanded.

"The Dark Fae have been more active of late. Not just the attack in New Orleans and here in the palace four years ago, but since. They've been gathering in other worlds, Aine."

"How so? The Concordant restricts the numbers of Fae, keeps them from sifting in large groups. That's why it was created — to stop armies of Fae from sifting elsewhere to make war."

The Donovan sighed. "Think about it, Aine."

Aine paled. "Rifts?"

"Yes. And it's stressing the fabric of space-time. I'm not sure how much longer before something very bad happens and they won't be able to close it. From our intelligence we know they haven't quite mastered the spell yet. They can only keep it open for brief periods of time, less than ten minutes. But they've been moving people and getting ready. This must be dealt with."

"She's coming, Jayce," one of the guards said quietly as he stood at the door.

"Mei, stand over there. Be silent until we draw her in. She will pay for this." Jayce pressed a quick, hard kiss on her lips and withdrew.

Eire came into the room all Fae magic and bouncy curls. As a child Mei had adored her aunt but her betrayal had killed all that and a murderous fury rode Mei's spine. To top it off the look she sent Jayce didn't escape Mei's attention. Jealous rage sliced through her at that look. She knew then another reason why Eire wanted her out of the way.

"What is it, Aine? You sent for me?" Eire's hair was golden, much like Mei's, her voice musical.

Freya put a hand on Mei's shoulder to keep her silent.

"Yes I did, sister. I wanted to talk with you about Mei. The anniversary of her...death is approaching and I always find myself so sad. Do you know someone came to me earlier today and told me my child was alive?"

Eire laughed prettily and then frowned. "Sister, do not let these rumors hurt you. She is gone. Dead on the battlefield, and you know I always said you were silly to let her go out there when she should have been here at your right hand. You could try to have another child. Or I could." Again the coy look at Jayce and Mei's eyes narrowed to slits.

Jayce stood, back stiff, one hand clasping the other wrist at his waist. His sword gleamed at his side.

Aine's jaw clenched a moment and then relaxed as she attempted to conceal her anger. "I hate to say this but the person, the one who told me Mei was alive, indicated that you knew this."

Eire put a hand to her throat in dismay. "Sister! How could you say such a thing to me? She is..."

"Alive and well apparently. Despite your attempts to the contrary." Aine stood and motioned for her guards to grab her sister.

"What is the meaning of this? I demand you let me go!"

Aine motioned at Mei to come forward.

"Hello, Aunt. How are you?" Mei's voice was edged with violence.

Eire froze and stared, pretty green eyes wide with shock. Actress that she was, she quickly fell back into her role. "Darling girl! You're alive. How can that be?" She turned to Aine. "Why do you have me held so that I cannot embrace my niece?"

"Do you think I would let your treachery come near my child again? Do you think I'm that much of a fool?"

"Treachery? Why, whatever can you mean, sister? You cannot think I had any part in harming her!"

"Send for Brian immediately." Aine didn't take her eyes from Eire as she issued the orders to her guards. "No one else is to come in or out of here."

"Tell me why you did it. It couldn't have been just for Jayce." Mei vibrated with rage, barely suppressing the urge to tear her aunt from limb to limb.

"Did what? Jayce?" Eire tried to move her gaze to Jayce.

Mei's hand shot out and grabbed Eire's throat. "Do *not* continue to play this. I spent a *thousand* years being tortured and raped. A thousand years! Every day I thought someone

17

would come for me but you never did. I finally got free and came here. And I spent two thousand more years thinking my mother exiled me and my lover was dead. You were the reason for at least two thousand of those years and if you do not tell me, you will die before anyone can get to you."

Eire's pulse sped as she began to struggle. Mei tightened her grip.

"Mei!" Jayce moved forward.

Mei's free hand shot out to stop him. "Do not move to save your bedmate, Jayce MacTavish! I will kill her if I need to and I won't shed a single tear."

"Don't do this. We need to find out why she did it. And damn it, I thought you were dead!"

"She will tell me or she will die. It matters not to me." Mei moved in so that she was nose to nose with her aunt. "You believe me, don't you? You know I'll kill you. So I'm going to loosen my grip before you pass out and you will tell me or die."

Mei loosened her hold but did not let go entirely and Jayce let out a breath.

Brian was escorted into the room and froze as Mei turned to face him.

Aine's audience chamber was spelled so that no use of Fae magic would work but her own. Mei knew they couldn't sift or shimmer away.

"You have a story to tell," Mei said to Eire, turning back to face her.

"You bitch!" Eire gasped for air and her hands moved to her neck, trying to pry Mei's grip loose. Unimpressed, Mei continued to hold her aunt's throat.

"Bitch doesn't begin to describe what I am. What you made me, Eire. Don't think about trying to best me. I'm stronger than you are and in here your magic is useless. You have nothing to fight me with. You're soft except for your black heart. Those years in Carthau made me very strong. And very ruthless. I am not the same woman who left to battle the dark ones that day in Sareem. That Mei is dead. Now talk or I will kill you with my bare hands."

"You'd better do what she says, Eire." Aine moved to sit on the throne.

"Or perhaps Brian has a tale for us." Freya moved forward a step.

Two guards held the seneschal but he made no attempt to fight or escape.

"Let me go or the Dark Fae will kill you all before taking the throne!"

Aine's brow went up at Eire's threat. "Is that so? And how would you know this?"

Mei rolled her eyes and gave Eire a quick jab in the kidney with her fist. "Eire, I believe I've told you what you need to do. That felt quite nice, I wouldn't mind giving you a dozen more. So start talking."

"You'll pay for this! Jayce, darling, how can you stand there while she does this to me?" Eire took great care to sound pitiful as she looked wide-eyed at Jayce.

"I'm not your darling. We've shared the sheets on and off over the years. She was…is my heart. And you betrayed us all. Tell us or she'll kill you. I think you can see it in her eyes."

"Did you know she was in Carthau?" Aine asked, her voice sharp.

"Yes! Yes, I did. They brought Jayce back with the few others who'd lived through the battle. One of the survivors told Brian that Mei had been taken." Eire stood up straight and proud and Mei backed up, letting her go. She wanted to hear the whole story and then she'd deal with her aunt's actions.

"Why didn't you tell me? Why didn't that survivor tell me? I don't understand!" Aine stood up and came to face her sister.

Eire snorted in disgust. "Because I had him killed. Really, Aine, you're so gullible you don't deserve the throne. I had him killed so I could tell you Mei had fallen at Sareem. Do you think I don't want to rule? And if she was around I couldn't have. And chances were she would be killed there anyway. It's a demon prison for goddess' sake! Who'd have thought she'd survive a thousand years there and break free?"

"But she did." The Donovan spoke then.

"Yes. And then she sifted near the gates and Brian saw her and sent for me. We had to think quickly but with Bron's help we were able to get the exile order and craft the spell. It was rather powerful. Even Mei believed her mother rejected her that day. Oh she cried and begged." Eire laughed at that.

"And I came back like nothing had changed." Eire looked from   Aine   to   Mei. "How? How did you get back here?"

"Did you think others of power would not know?" the Donovan asked.

"If you did, why wait so long?"

Mei thought that was a very good question, one she planned to follow up on with The Donovan herself when the time was right.

The Donovan shrugged. "Mine isn't to reason why. I found out of her existence and we sent in people to help her escape. She came to you and you rejected her and she came back to me. She's been with me ever since. Training. But you know why I'm here now, don't you?"

"It doesn't matter if you know. You can't kill me without a trial of the full ruling council. Give me the throne and none of this will be necessary. Our armies will have no need to attack Tir na nOg." Eire's head was held high. She had balls, Mei had to give her that.

"Oh sure, why not? And Earth? We know how much you love Earth," Mei sneered.

"Earth has to go. Humans are a blight and they should no longer be tolerated. We waste our time and magic protecting them." Eire lifted her shoulders nonchalantly.

"Hmm. How about you fuck off? The warriors can find the Dark Fae elsewhere and kill them until they exist no more. I think that's a far better deal than giving you the throne and letting them slay humanity. Maybe we can even send you to Carthau." Mei leaned in, satisfied to see Eire flinch slightly.

"Who is your contact here? Who else is involved?" Jayce asked, moving Mei aside. She kept Eire within reach.

"As if you were good enough in bed to tell you that." Eire snorted.

"Take her to the holding room. We have people who can do this without strangulation," Jayce called to his second, Cullen.

"You will not!" Mei inserted herself in between Eire and Jayce. "You will not protect her from me! I will have justice and she will tell us what we need to know."

Jayce took her shoulders in gentle hands. "*A thaisce*, do you think I'd do anything to hurt you? This is not just about you. It's about finding the conspirators living among us. You know the danger of rift magic. We can't risk you killing her before we find out the whole of it."

"He's right, Mei. He's doing his job." The Donovan touched her shoulder. "Let him do it. You will get justice, sweetpea. In due time."

"In due time? How about three thousand years. Is that due time enough? Oh it's all well and good for me to have to put everyone else first but what about me? Huh? I'm supposed to put these people first when they left me in Carthau to rot?"

Jayce closed his eyes a moment. "Mei, I can't even think straight right now. I'm so shocked and overjoyed to have you back. But this has to happen my way. You've gotten enough information from her for now. She can't escape from the holding room. We'll put Brian in another one and send for the people who can get the truth from them both."

"Please, Mei." Aine spoke softly in the background and Mei threw up her arms and moved away from Jayce and Eire.

"Fine."

Cullen stuck his head out and sent for more guards and in moments they showed up. If they were shocked to see Mei and to escort the next in line to the throne to the Fae version of a jail cell, none showed it.

"I need to set up a stronger guard here around the queen's quarters." Jayce stood and went to the door. He turned to Mei before leaving. "Please don't leave. I want to know you again. I'll be back as soon as I can."

"I...it's very complicated, Jayce."

He nodded. "I expect it is. But will you wait? We can work through it, I know we can."

Mei didn't know what to do but she nodded that she'd stay and he smiled before he left the room to deal with Eire.

"Carissa, have Mei's rooms readied immediately. We'll have to have an announcement very soon that she's back and also that my sister has been arrested for acting in collusion with the Dark Fae." Aine reached out and took Mei's hand. "You'll stay, won't you? I mean, for good?"

Mei sighed. "I have commitments elsewhere. I'm with someone. I don't know what to say here." Seeing Jayce again had shot straight to her heart. Their bond was so strong that she'd never stopped loving him. But she had Card. Confusion washed through her. Card was her partner. And her husband. He'd watched her back for the last two thousand years and it was impossible to imagine her life without him.

But she couldn't live without Jayce. She loved Jayce. Loved him and needed him in a way that she couldn't begin to quantify. The thought of him had kept her alive through things she could never have survived otherwise.

Her hesitancy about it must have shown on her face because her mother interrupted her thoughts. "Darling, he has mourned you every day of the last three thousand years. Yes, he's had others in his bed. I imagine you have too. But he did not take Eire's side just now. He did his job and it just about killed him to have to leave to deal with her."

Mei shrugged. "I don't want to talk about that. But as for my life between then and now I haven't had others. One other. One very big bad shifter who is not going to be pleased."

Aine laughed. "A shifter, hmm? Well, you do have good taste. Surely he'll understand about all of this? Even if you're breaking things off with him?"

"I'm not breaking things off with him. Mother, he's my husband. I'm mated to him. And I love him. He's half Were, half demon. They both take this stuff seriously. He and I spoke the bond. He's my other half."

Aine exhaled sharply. "And what of your bond with Jayce? You were with him first."

"It's not gone. He still burns in my heart but it's been several thousand years and my bond with Card exists as well. And I've been with Card for two thousand years. Longer than I was with Jayce."

It was the Donovan's turn to laugh. "Card is not the understanding type. But he will want the best for Mei. And if he believes Jayce is what's right for her, he'll work to help find a solution to this problem."

"Do you think Jayce is what's right for me?" Mei turned to look at her boss.

"Only you, Card and Jayce can decide that one."

Mei tossed her arms into the air. "Oh I hate when you do that. Go all Matrix Oracle on me. At least shoot me a cookie when you do it."

"You're not nearly as scary when you're dressed like that. I quite like all that skin showing."

"I can conjure up some biker boots if you like."

The Donovan laughed. "I'm sure you could, sweetpea. But for now I'll deal with Card and you stay here. I will bring him along in a while. Remember the time slip. This issue of rifts must be dealt with, it is of utmost importance that they are stopped."

"Please tell him I love him and I have no intention of trying to sever our bond. This is going hurt him enough without feeling uncertainty about where my loyalty lies."

The Donovan nodded.

Freya kissed both Mei's cheeks.

Aine grabbed Freya into a hug. "Thank you both for returning her to me. Carl, you and I will have words about this later on."

"My beautiful queen, I will be back in several hours' time. But you may not throw things at my head." He winked and she growled.

The two bowed and walked out, leaving Mei with her mother and two guards. "You need more Favored in here. Don't kid yourself that by now the word hasn't made it to their spies. The Dark Fae will know and want to make their move to either free Eire or kill her. And if you're in the way to either one, you're a target."

"Come through to my quarters. We'll have tea and you will rest."

"Mother, do I have my rank back?"

Aine stilled and turned in the doorway. "Yes, of course, darling. It was never taken from you to begin with."

Mei turned to the Favored in the room. "Cian, right?

The dark-haired guard nodded. "Welcome home, princess." He bowed his head.

"Thank you. Please go and get four more guards. Post two at each doorway."

"Right away." He obeyed without even looking at Aine so Mei was sure he'd heard her mother tell her she had her rank back, making her second-in-command.

Aine inclined her head and waved Mei through to her personal quarters. Once inside, Mei stopped. The room was pretty much exactly the same as it'd been the last time she'd been there. The morning she'd left for Sareem. Except a small shrine sat on a corner table. A shrine to Mei.

"I told you I mourned your loss." Aine put her head on Mei's shoulder and looked at the shrine, where a picture of Mei as a child dominated, surrounded by flowers and small bits and pieces of Mei's childhood. A bracelet, some silly clay bits and bobs she'd made by hand for her mother.

"I don't know what to say. I woke up this morning and things were the same way they'd been for over three thousand years and now they're all different and I don't know what to do."

"Sit down. Drink." Aine waved a hand and the empty tea table on the other side of the room was suddenly heavy with food and a steaming pot of tea. "I conjured extra coconut cakes for you."

Mei turned to her mother, tears in her eyes, and hugged her.

"Oh baby, I've missed you so. It's such a gift, a blessing to have you back here with me. I can't quite believe it. It feels like a dream and I'm terrified I'll wake up and the piece of my heart that ran around this palace like a terror will be gone again. But one thing I know for sure, I love you. I always have and I always will. You must believe that I had nothing to do with your exile."

A dam of emotion broke through Mei then. Great sobs poured out of her as her mother smoothed a hand over her hair and murmured soothing words.

* * * * *

Jayce approached Aine's quarters, his mind on the details of setting up a greater guard presence as well as on all that had happened in the last hours.

His hands shook as he pulled the chain he always wore from under his shirt. His wedding band hung from it. It hadn't left his body since the day he'd finally taken it off five hundred years after he'd been told she died at Sareem. By that bitch Eire.

Shame burned through him that he'd slept with her. Enjoyed her in bed many times. He'd certainly never been in love with her, or anyone else but Mei for that matter. But he felt like a traitor for sleeping with the woman who'd done so much harm to Mei. Hell, to their entire race!

Seeing Mei again after so many years had been like a fist to the gut. She'd been one of the most beautiful women he'd ever seen and was even more so now. She'd been two thousand years old when she'd gone. The Fae hit a maturing period when they turned three thousand years or so. Grew into their features more, lost the softness of youth and gained more definition of face and form. The woman who'd stood there in her familial colors, hair tumbling down her back and shoulders in rivers of curls shot with silver cording to hold it away from her face—that was a woman. A woman who'd seen more than he would have ever wished for anyone to see.

A thousand years in the most brutal prison in creation. A prison on the outskirts of hell itself run by demons and lesser demons known as darklings. He wanted to fall and beat his chest at what she must have suffered. Felt like a failure for not going to rescue her himself. She suffered while he lived and fucked and fought and laughed.

And how could she not blame him?

He saw two guards on the outer and then inner doors to Aine's private chambers and nodded. "Good. I'm glad to see you take the initiative, Cian. They're inside? Has anyone come?"

"The princess ordered it so, sir. And yes, they're inside. Many people have approached within the last twenty minutes. I believe the news has traveled through Tir na nOg by now. Carissa has come and gone twice. There will be an Audience in half an hour."

"Someone needs to let Conchobar know. I'll deal with that in a bit." Cian moved back and let Jayce pass, nodding as Jayce spoke. It would be up to Aine to tell Con he had a sister. Boy, that one had been a surprise. They'd always been told Mei's father was an unnamed noble. And, well, Jayce supposed that was true. Con had loved Mei like a sister and Jayce knew he'd be glad of the news. Titania on the other hand would not. He shook it off. One thing at a time. She was alive. *Alive!*

He knocked and then entered, stopping for a moment when he saw the mother and daughter sitting together on a chaise, Mei's head on Aine's shoulder as they drank tea. It was obvious by the red eyes that both had been crying.

They looked up at him as he entered. As if by rote, he went to Mei's side, needing to be near her, to reassure himself that she wouldn't simply disappear.

"There's to be an Audience in thirty minutes. And then I want you to take Mei home to rest. Your old quarters here have been readied for you both. She captured a darkling earlier today after chasing it for a week. She needs sleep."

"Mother, I'm fine. I'm five thousand years old. I can take care of myself you know. I've hunted demons and feral vampires and all manner of dark and evil things for the last two thousand years.."

"And I, darling girl, am tens of thousands of years old. I know more than you do and I'm queen, so there. You will rest and have time alone with Jayce. Let's do this Audience first."

"Tell me how my father and brothers died first."

Aine blinked. "Nessa was murdered by the Dark Fae, the son of Aillen whom Nessa had executed for murdering humans. But Conchobar and Finn aren't dead. Eire told you that too?"

"I never got to tell him." Mei closed her eyes and without thinking Jayce reached out and took her hand, bringing it to his lips.

"He would have been pleased, you know. He did like you, thought you were a firecracker. Used to tease Con that he was a stupid boy for letting me snatch you up first. Guess that was a good thing, huh?"

Mei looked up at him and he felt part of their connection flow through him once more. His body came to life at her nearness.

"But you will tell Con and Finn and both will be so pleased. I know this."

"Do you think? They won't be ashamed of me?"

"If they are, neither is the man I thought them to be!" Aine sputtered. "I'm sorry, Mei. I should have told him. He always suspected of course, but I fudged the times around, told him I was already pregnant when he and I had our, er, tryst. He had enough guilt over it and I didn't wish to ruin his marriage to Titania. She didn't deserve him but neither did I." Aine pushed a curl out of Mei's face. "But you did, and I'm sorry."

"Where are they? I'd like to see both of them soon."

"Conchobar lives on Earth half the time with his wife Emily, a Charvez witch and a transformed Fae. Oh and their daughter, Elise. If Earth time hasn't sped up a hundred years or anything, I saw them about a week ago. For Elise's first birthday. Finn lives here, near The Great Meadow, with his wife Magda and their two sons. We'll go see them soon, I promise." He paused. "We'll talk more when we're alone. There's so much to say, so much to know. Goddess I've missed you, Mei."

She nodded, turning her body into his, letting him hold her, letting the sound of his heart comfort her. "I need to tell you something, Jayce."

Carissa came into the room. "It's time for the Audience."

Aine stood. "I'll be waiting near the door. We can't delay."

Mei nodded and looked back to Jayce. "I don't even know if you still want me or what my return means to you."

Jayce interrupted her by kissing her hard. "Is that what you worried about? Mei, I love you. I've not stopped loving you. I haven't been celibate but I didn't know. I swear to you on my life, I didn't know."

Mei squeezed his hand. "I do believe you. At first I wasn't sure but I am now. And I love you too. But it's not that simple. I haven't been celibate either."

"I didn't expect you would have been. I understand, Mei. I do."

"Well, you may not be so understanding in a minute. I'm mated, Jayce."

His face paled and she rushed on.

"My bond with you still lives in my heart. I feel it, have felt it every day for three thousand years. But I thought you were dead as you thought I was. I'd been exiled."

"I..." He shook his head. "I don't know what to say. What do you want to do?"

"I'm sorry, we need to get moving," Aine called from the door.

"I've lived in exile for three thousand years, I will take this time right now. Period." She looked to her mother for long moments and then back to Jayce once Aine nodded.

"It's really up to you and Card. You need to know I love you. It kept me alive those centuries in Carthau. My memories freed me, let me go far away when..." Her voice wavered and Jayce made a low sound of anguish and kissed her softly.

"I love you too." He pulled his wedding band out of his shirt and showed it to her. "I kept it with me every moment."

"They took mine."

"It doesn't matter. Look, Mei, I can't lie and say I'm not shocked and off balance. And we have a lot to do right this very moment. But I'm not going to walk away without trying to make this work."

"Even if you have to share me with another?"

He took a deep breath. "I don't know how we'll do it. I don't. But I want you to know I want to work it out if we can."

"That's enough for now."

Jayce stood and held his arm out. Mei placed a hand on it and leaned into him as he pressed a kiss to her temple. With a quick adjustment her hair was perfect and clothes unwrinkled.

"You look beautiful. Shall we go?"

Chapter Two

ℵ

Card looked up from the baseball game when the Donovan suddenly appeared in the room. He was the only being that could have gotten through the wards unapproved.

"Just come on in, don't worry about knocking. Where's Mei?" Card turned the game off and tossed the remote to the table his feet rested on.

"She's in Tir na nOg."

Card came to his feet so fast the Donovan barely even saw the movement. "She's where? Is she in danger? I'll grab my weapons and we can go."

The Donovan folded his frame into the chair across from the couch. "Sit down. She's not in danger." He told Card the whole story of the rifts, the Dark Fae and the betrayal.

"She's got to be gutted. I should go to her."

"Well, yes. You should and we will. But first I need to talk to you about one last thing. Jayce isn't dead."

Card's face darkened. "And what does that mean? Is she with him now?"

The Donovan took in the other man carefully. He looked human. Mostly. But he wasn't. Not even a smidgen. He was half werewolf, half demon, but you wouldn't know it most of the time. Most of the time he was the kind of man many people would think was a cop. Square jaw, brown-blond hair that hit his collar, wary, otherworldly steel-gray eyes. The man was built like a tank, broad, muscular. And he adored Mei with a fervor and depth that Carl Donovan had only seen less than a handful of times in his long existence.

"She is with her mother. And yes, Jayce is there. But Card, she wants me to bring you there and she wanted me to tell you that she loves you and has no intention of trying to sever your bond. She doesn't want you to have any uncertainty about where her loyalty lies."

"But she still loves him and the Fae marriage bond doesn't go away. It must still affect her."

"She and Jayce are not fated ones, that's extremely rare. But they did a mating ceremony and that includes a bond. Much like the one she did with you. So yes, she does still love him. I'm sorry to have to tell you this."

Card's fist hit the couch cushions so hard it plunged out the back. "What am I supposed to do with this? She's my wife. My woman. My mate! I've loved her every moment of the last two thousand years, ever since I saw her chained to the floor of her cell at Carthau. I'm not giving her up, I don't care if he had her first."

"May I give you some advice?"

The eyes Card turned to the Donovan had bled into a gray that sparkled metallic. The eyes of his demon mother. He nodded, trying to get himself under control.

"Card, she loves you. There isn't a single doubt in my mind that she does. If pressed she will choose you and come back here and live her old life again. And you'd be happy for a time. But it would be there. The life she had before and was robbed of. Her mother, her destiny to lead the Fae, her home in Tir na nOg. Would you want to take that from her? To hold her when you already have her?"

"And then what, Carl? Do I spend Monday, Wednesday and Friday with her and her other man gets the rest of the week? We alternate Sundays? I live here and she lives there? I get a shadow of her love and attention?"

Shaking his head, the Donovan sighed. "No. It would be easiest if you lived in Tir na nOg as well. I don't think she plans on stopping her work as a warrior and you two can do it from there. Time is handled easier from that side of the veil and right now there are serious doings and she'll need you at her side. Share her. Is it optimal? Probably not. But you can't give her up and she doesn't want to give you up and she's bonded to him too.

"The truth is that none of this is the fault of you three but it is an inescapable truth. She is bonded to two men. The way you feel about her? She feels it for you and for him too. As he feels for her. I've spoken with Freya in depth about this and there's something I can do if you're willing."

The Donovan began to explain.

* * * * *

Aine walked out first, flanked by her Favored, but she insisted Jayce stay with Mei, which was fine with both of them.

A collective gasp and shocked whispers filled the room as they all entered and were seen.

Mei had forgotten how beautiful the Fae were. Bits and pieces of her memory began to return after the millennia away from her own kind. As they spoke in hushed tones she heard bits of laughter here and there. Their voices were seductive and musical. The women were tall and stunning in all shapes and hues. The men ranged from lithe and athletic to broad and heavily muscled. Most had hair just past their shoulders and a very few had very long hair with the warrior braids at the temple.

Mei could see joy, curiosity, anger, jealousy and even fear on the faces they passed. Suddenly a woman stood forward in their path. Mei's body tightened, ready for defense, and Jayce moved forward slightly.

"Majesty, it's true then?"

"Sorcha, yes. My daughter has returned." Aine's voice rang clear over the murmuring and the room got very quiet.

The blonde looked Mei up and down. "Are you sure? What of the fact that the girl died? This woman could be any interloper out to steal the throne. We know Dark Fae are about."

The murmuring rose again until Aine put her hand up to silence them all. "In the first place, Sorcha, are you questioning my judgment? That would be unwise no matter who your mother is."

Sorcha must have known enough to fear Aine's wrath because she shook her head vehemently. "Of course not, Majesty!"

"Good, I'll take it you're *concerned* for my welfare then. Several things make me believe this is my child. First, I know my child. I birthed her, I raised her. I know her mannerisms and her voice and face. As do many of you, including her own husband." Aine indicated Jayce, who nodded and looked at Mei with a smile.

"Second, Freya and the Donovan brought her to me."

The room erupted in whispers again and quieted just as quickly when Aine raised a hand. "Lastly," Aine turned to Mei, "please turn."

Mei, knowing what her mother meant to do, nodded and turned her body so her back was to the crowd. Aine lifted her hair. She'd had the mark her whole life. Had to hide it for many years but it was one thing she'd never forgotten. Her mother had told her the mark would always be her link to her family and the throne. Hearing the collective gasp of the crowd, Mei figured her mother had been right.

"Most importantly, she bears the mark of my family. The women in my line all have this mark, as you know. She is my blood. And your future queen." Aine turned Mei around and pulled her to her side.

Any doubt she'd seen on faces was now gone. Yes, many faces showed distrust and anger, but they all believed she was Mei NiaAine.

They filed up to the dais and sat. Mei took her seat at her mother's right hand and Jayce stood next to her, hand on his sword hilt, the other on the back of her chair, his fingertips just brushing her shoulder.

Aine held up a hand and the room silenced immediately. She then told them all the story of Mei's disappearance and who had been behind it. Chaos broke out as people began to truly realize that the sister of the queen had betrayed them all. It warred with the joy at Mei's return.

"We will do an Audience each day, just as we did before. I want to ask everyone to simply be more alert and aware of your surroundings as we continue to investigate just how deep this treachery goes. Now Mei is tired and we're all in need of rest after such an emotional day. Please respect her privacy just now. I know you're all glad to have her back among us but let her get used to us again. Any appointments will go through Carissa for now."

Without letting any further questions be asked, Aine stood and they exited the chamber.

"You two go on now. Spend some time. Those quarters are the safest in the palace next to mine. I'll see you in the morning." Aine hugged Mei tight and turned to Jayce. "And you, until I say otherwise you will be the chief of Mei's personal guard. Of course you'll retain your status as my chief councilor but she needs you more than I do right now."

Jayce bowed. "Thank you, Majesty. I've doubled your personal guard. Each one is someone I'd trust with my life."

She thanked him and Jayce drew Mei through two sets of connecting doors and into the foyer of what had long been their apartments at the palace.

Card, the Donovan and Freya waited in the living room.

Upon seeing Card there, Mei's heart leapt and she moved to him quickly, into his arms. Relief poured through her that he held her tight and true.

"You're looking beautiful as always, precious. So, quite a kerfuffle you've wandered into." He kissed her softly and set her back from him, looking her up and down.

"Donovan told you everything?" She looked back at Jayce, who stood in the doorway looking angry and vulnerable.

"You must be Jayce." Card held his hand out to shake. "Mei spoke of you often. I can't say I'm fond of the circumstances but I am glad to hear you're not dead after all."

Sighing, Jayce moved forward and shook Card's hand. "You would have to be straight up and true for a woman like Mei to love you so much."

"My, aren't you civil." Freya's melodic voice had humor in it. "And oh, isn't this awkward? Shall we all sit down? Carl and I have found something that may help the three of you in this transition."

Mei sat on a long couch and Card took one side and Jayce the other.

"I spoke with Card about this earlier this evening so I know his feelings but let me tell you what we propose and you can accept or not. You two males are each bonded magically and emotionally to the same woman. As it happens both bonds are very strong. The Fae binding ritual and the Were ritual are very old and there's no way around that. Even when Jayce and Mei each thought the other dead they still loved each other and the only reason it was possible for them to move forward was because they thought the other was dead.

"Freya and I have been around awhile." The Donovan winked at Freya. "And we've learned a few things and have some pretty strong magic of our own. Freya has located a very old spell that would bind the three of you together. Essentially it would take the magic that each spell created and bind it into a third spell, one that united the three of you into a bond."

"Why would you do this?" Jayce asked.

"Because Mei is someone I love very much. I feel partially responsible for this situation as I knew you were alive when she and Card performed their bond. I could not tell her and..." The Donovan broke off, unable to speak, and emotion welled up within Mei as she remembered how devastated and emotionally broken she'd been after her time in Carthau. She'd needed Card's love so much and he'd given it to her without expecting anything in return.

The Donovan continued. "This would enable the three of you to be united in a way that would make it much easier to be together as a triad. A Fae male and a man like Card, half Were, half demon, would not be able to share a mated female easily. I cannot see that it would end well. But this spell would enable all of you to share a relationship of three parts."

"Would the feeling of being threatened ease?" Jayce asked, his hand squeezing Mei's.

"I think so, yes." Freya leaned forward from her perch on the chair arm. "You have this connection to Mei now, correct?"

Jayce nodded. "I can feel her. I realize now that I always could, just a whisper. Probably because of the distance. I had nightmares, terrible ones." His voice broke a moment. "I imagine it was what she was enduring in Carthau. And it always felt like she was with me in some way or another. I suppose she was. Just not how I'd imagined it. But now she is here." He put a palm over his heart. "Where she lodged the day we said those vows. In my veins."

Freya turned to Card. "And you?"

"Always. She is my everything."

"Well, you two will feel this way about each other too. In a very concrete sense you will be Card's mate too, Jayce, and the other way around, Card. I don't know how much that will, er, translate. But I do know the binding will be of three and not two."

"How do you feel about this, Mei?" Card asked.

"I'm selfish. I know that. I want you both. I love you both. But I don't want you to be hurt or do something you don't want to. The bond is real and it's forever and it's not something I want you to undertake," she looked toward Jayce for a moment, "either of you, unless you want it."

"I want it. I want it to make this ache go away. I've been trying to think of how we'd endure this and I didn't know how. But if I can enjoy your happiness at being reunited with your first husband instead of feeling this terrible jealous anger, if I can still love and be loved by you and be happy? I choose that." Card kissed her forehead and she leaned in to him for a moment.

"And you, Jayce?"

"Polyamory isn't unheard of among the Fae. You know this yourself. And Card is right. I want you to be happy too and I know right now you're dealing with a lot of conflicting feelings. I'd like to think I'd have tried very hard to make it work between all of us but truthfully, I'm not sure how it would have. Would I prefer it be just you and me? Yes. I would. But it can't be and I won't wish it away because that would wish you away and wish away your happiness for the last two thousand years. I love you too much to want that. I vote we do this."

"So is this unanimous?" Freya stood.

Each one of them nodded.

"Come then, let us do this now. We should be outside so I'll take you to my favorite place."

When they took Freya's hand and touched her arm, they sifted into a meadow overlooking a clear blue lake with a large hall at the top of the hill.

"The Hall of the Gods." Card took it in, impressed.

"Indeed. You know your history, Card."

He shrugged.

"Kneel. Mei, you in the middle. Jayce, do you have something from your mating to Mei? A ring, a handkerchief, something like that?"

Jayce pulled the chain and the ring over his head, handing it to Freya. Without being asked, Card held out his ring and Mei hers.

"I don't have my ring from my and Jayce's mating anymore."

"That is fine. A bit of your blood will do." Freya looked into Mei's eyes as she sliced across Mei's forearm and spilled the blood over the rings. She then drew a sigil over the heart and on the forehead of each person and told them to hold hands.

The language Freya spoke was old. Older than recorded time. Powerful. Mei felt it begin to tug on her senses, her will and perception. Each man squeezed her hands tight. With her last words Freya's hands rose up to the sky and then quickly moved to point down and it felt like a lightning bolt shot through her body.

Mei lost all sense of time and space for long moments, a total disconnect, and then she slowly floated back into her body. And when she opened her eyes and consciousness returned, it was there. That ember of the bond she'd had with each man was a full-burning flame.

"Wow." Card looked at Mei and then over to Jayce, who nodded.

"I can feel you both. This is actually more intense than the Fae bond."

"I think it simply amplified the different magic and then wove it into one strand. The spell created something totally new. It worked then for you, Mei?" Freya asked.

Mei nodded. "I can't explain it right now. But the bond is more than just with me at the center point. It's a connection of all of us."

"You should go back and get to know each other. You have trials and tribulations ahead. The unification of three hearts and souls also unified your magic. Again, something new. Fae magic tinged with Were and demon magic. This will serve you well in your...in what you will face."

"Donovan, what aren't you saying?" Mei asked, standing up.

"Oh cupcake, if I told you it wouldn't be as much fun. And you know I'm just going to cite the rules. Go on back. I'll see you soon."

And with a flick of his wrist Mei, Jayce and Card stood in their living room back at the palace.

"I hate it when he does that," Card murmured.

"I take it he pops in often?" Jayce looked at Mei.

"Now and again. Card and I work for him. You know there are bad things in the universes, he comes to set us on them. I expect that after we deal with the Dark Fae he'll find something new to pester us about."

The feeling shifted and suddenly Mei was nervous. More nervous than she'd been the first time she'd ever had sex or the first time after Carthau.

Card reached out and caressed the line of her jaw, easing her tension. "Precious, don't be nervous. It's just me. And it's not like you haven't had sex with both of us before."

Jayce laughed. "Get right to the point, don't you, Card?"

"I'm a blunt man. I don't believe in beating around the bush. I'm hungry for her. You are too I expect. It's been three thousand years for you. For me it was just this morning. In an alley, against a brick wall. Wasn't it?" A smile curved up one side of his mouth, making Mei shiver. The memory of how he'd taken her, hard and fast, like he couldn't last another moment without touching her, flowed through her.

The air thickened with sexual tension as the three of them pondered the possibilities.

"So, uh, how is this going to work? You're both okay with this?" Mei's voice shook a bit.

"Whatever the hell Freya did and said, it made me more than okay. I expect Card and I will have to work around each other for a bit to work out the kinks." Jayce moved to stand right behind her and spoke in her ear. "Or perhaps we'll keep the kinks in. I think I may find out all sorts of new and interesting things about you."

"Is that your sword hilt?"

It was Card's turn to laugh then. "Your sense of humor is back. You feelin' okay, then?"

"More than okay. I gotta tell you both, this is um, pretty hot. It's like I'm in your heads, both of you. Your arousal is something I can feel like it's my own. I can tell it's not mine, but it's there inside me like you both are. It adds a lot to the experience."

"Do you still like to take long baths and showers?" Jayce nuzzled her neck and shivers broke over her.

"Yes. And I should. It's been a long day. Week."

Jayce moved around her body, holding a hand out to her. "Let's go then. If the shower stall isn't big enough for three we'll simply make it bigger."

Mei took his hand and held her other out to Card and the three of them walked down the hall to the cavernous bathroom.

"Before things get too involved, I'm going to go be sure the guards are on the right schedule and that they know Card is here now." Jayce pressed a kiss to her fingertips. "I'll be back in a few minutes. Don't get too far ahead." Winking, he turned and left, leaving Mei alone with Card.

"You think he did that on purpose?" Card pulled his shirt off and Mei moaned softly at the exposed muscle of his upper body. Even after nearly two thousand years he still made her want to lick him from head to toe every time she saw him. "Thank you. I feel better now." He cocked his head and smiled.

She touched his chest greedily, smoothing her hands over his skin, loving the way he felt. "For what? And he's the head of the Favored, which means he thinks about this stuff all the time. So part of it was real. Even before when he was lower in rank he was like this. But he's very thoughtful so it may have been a way to leave us alone for a few minutes too."

41

"Thank you for still looking at me like you want to devour me."

His hands skimmed over her neck, down the line of her arms and cradled her ass. The heat began to build in his touch.

"Card Leviathan, I love you. I've loved you since the moment you burst into my cell and broke me free of those chains. I loved you when you were so shy asking me to be your mate that you actually stuttered. I love that you were willing to be bonded to my first husband to make me happy and I'm really happy that you seem to be okay with the bond too. I *do* want to devour you. But I'd rather have you inside me just now."

His mouth found hers as his hands moved to the fastenings on the gown. Cool air hit her bare back and then her legs as the silk pooled at her feet. His lips were hot, urgent, and she opened to the slick insistence of his tongue as it slid into her mouth, stroking against her own.

His taste roared through her and she pressed herself to him as tightly as possible. The kiss started slow and sensual and built in intensity until Mei felt as if she were drowning in him and all she could do was hang on for the ride.

The first time he'd kissed her, it started out as a comfort. Eleven years after Carthau and she'd still had nightmares. She'd still mourned the loss of her family and Jayce. They'd been on the beach off the Oregon Coast and the sunset had been so beautiful it made her ache.

With gentle hands he'd turned her to face him and kissed her cheeks, tasting her tears. Slowly, making sure she had enough time to call a halt, he'd moved to her mouth and with the softest, gentlest brush of his lips, had kissed her.

She knew then that he was someone she could trust. That he would protect her and care for her but most of all, he'd respect her. Mei had already pretty much fallen in love with him but that gentle kiss had been the moment she'd let herself go and stopped feeling guilty for wanting a new start.

Her hands dropped to the waist of his jeans, her fingers tracing around just inside, denim to bare skin. The scent of his desire tickled her senses, seducing her. Unable to resist looking, she stood back a step when she undid his pants, smiling when his cock spilled out into her hands. "I love your cock," she said, bringing her thumb, slick with pre-cum, to her mouth.

"God, I love it when you do that. You're so damned sexy." Card's eyes glittered as he watched. Pressing one last kiss to her lips, he added, "I love you too, Mei. I needed to hear all that. I felt it, but I needed to hear it too."

She felt the emotion there between them and it caught in her throat for a moment.

The sound of a throat being cleared brought them both around. In the background, Card started the water in the shower. Jayce strode back in to the room, gaze intent on Mei's body. "Goddess, you're more beautiful now than you were three thousand years ago."

Mei's mouth dried and her eyes widened as Jayce magicked his clothing away. It wasn't so much that she'd forgotten how beautiful he was, but it had been tucked away as a sweet memory that hurt too much to dwell on. Where Card was just under six feet tall and all broad, wide muscle, Jayce was nearly seven feet tall. His arms were muscled from swordwork, his belly flat from weapons drills and training. Fiery red hair hung down his back to his waist, the braids of the Favored at each temple. When they were younger she'd been so impressed by the older warriors and now Jayce was one. *Her* Jayce was one.

"I'm beautiful? Jayce, the two of you make me want to fall to my knees and shout thanks to the heavens."

Wearing a sexy, arrogant grin, he reached out, grabbed her hand and pulled her into his arms, his mouth finding hers.. It had been so long and the shock of recognition slammed into her as she clung to him while he plundered her mouth. Tears of joy and homecoming pricked her lashes.

"I'm the one who's thankful. To have you back with me after I thought I'd lost you forever? What a blessed man I am."

Jayce picked her up and automatically her legs wrapped about his waist as he carried her into the shower where Card already waited, steam rising from his body.

"Okay, shower first and then fucking. Lots of fucking." Jayce kissed her tears away before putting her down under the spray. "So beautiful. You were this memory I carried inside me for so long. Sometimes I wondered if it'd ever been real." He slid soap-slicked hands over her as Card helped with her hair. "And yet here you are, the same woman and yet different. But it's good. And I'm seeing this other man touch you and instead of being pissed off, it turns me on. I can't say I've ever been attracted to men or had voyeur fantasies but it works." He winked at Card over Mei's shoulder and they shared a laugh.

"Oh man, you two are going to double team me? Oh, wait, that doesn't sound bad. I take it back if it sounded like a complaint." Mei arched into Jayce's touch as he palmed her nipples. Tug and pinch, over and over until unconsciously she rolled her hips into his body.

"Please, let's get out of here. I'm not proud, I'm begging you. Two men, two cocks, four hands, someone needs to be using them on me, and right now!"

Laughing, it only took a matter of moments before everyone was clean and dry and practically running back to the bedroom. Kissing and petting, they all fell to the bed in a tangle of arms and legs.

Jayce trailed his tongue down her neck and to her breasts. On the other side, Card moved between her thighs, kissing up the inside. Jayce smiled as the edge of his teeth dragged over the sensitive nipple, bringing a moan from her lips.

"Well, some things don't change, I'm glad to see. You still have the prettiest, sexiest breasts a woman ever carried. I wonder, can I still make you come just by playing with them?"

Card chuckled just before his tongue flicked out to drag over her clit.

"Okay, well, you know, we can test that another time. But right now, someone needs to be... Oh yes, that works." Mei hissed as Card got down to business, his mouth on her pussy. The demon side of him came out during sex and his temperature rose—the heat of him was an indicator of just how turned on he was. She also knew he'd keep her dancing on the edge of orgasm for hours if he chose, his magic holding her there or pushing her into climax after climax depending on his mood.

With a last tug on her nipple with his teeth, Jayce got to his knees, looking down the line of her body. The intensity of her beauty had always touched him deeply. Long legs, curves for miles, muscles where there should be, feminine softness everywhere else. Her breasts were still sexy and went with the gentle flare of her hips. The impact now though was doubled by the contrast of that intensely gorgeous femininity with the places that marked her time at the hands of the demons at Carthau. Scars ran over her torso and thighs along with burn marks. As Fae she would have healed from most things except wounds made with cold iron and burns. They'd marked her intentionally. Rage began to bubble up, along with guilt. She'd suffered all of that while he did nothing to help her.

Feeling his anger through their connection, Mei's eyes opened as she looked up at him. "Yes. These are from my time at Carthau." Running a self-conscious hand over her side, she blushed. "Not as pretty as other Fae females, I know."

He kissed one long scar from hip to breast. "You are more beautiful than any other female I've ever beheld. This is just a scar, Mei. A mark of someone else's depravity. It doesn't lessen you."

"Amen. I've been telling her that for years. I'm proud to say my mother broke away from her tribe and settled into my father's pack. Not all of us are butchers." Card spoke, a mixture of tenderness and defensiveness apparent in his voice.

It touched and gladdened Jayce that Card adored Mei so much.

"I know that because Mei was with you, you had to be honorable. You saved her where I did not. I am in your debt."

Card nodded, the defensiveness sliding away from his face.

Jayce's gaze went back to Mei, who stared at his cock hungrily. "Since you're looking at it, I think you should suck my cock. Let me feel your mouth around me once again."

Card moved so that Mei could rise to her knees. Moving to Jayce, she ran her hands over his scalp, his hair like fire against her creamy skin. He'd almost forgotten how she loved his hair, how she used to wrap it around herself. Memories of her, of them together, awoke within him.

Her lips pressed a line down his body as her golden hair trailed over his skin. The line of her spine curved as she moved toward his cock and when her mouth reached him electricity shot through his veins. It seemed unreal to have her again. She'd been dead to him for three thousand years and yet there she was, the greatest gift he'd ever received. Twice.

"Lie back," she said, pulling her mouth away from him.

He moved to comply and she scrambled over his body, her pretty ass up in the air as her head dipped down to take him back into her mouth.

"Now there's a sight I can appreciate." Card moved behind her, his hands caressing the length of her spine before moving to stroke her pussy from behind.

Jayce watched Card touch Mei and it was hotter than just about anything he'd ever seen. Watching Card, his mate, touch Mei, the woman they both loved so much, connected them in a continuum of longing. Card's desire became his desire, he felt it like his own, only with a slight difference in flavor. Card's hunger was tinged with the feral nature of his origins.

Mei's mouth rose and fell on his cock, her tongue swirling and flicking around the head. He fell deeper and deeper into her spell with each swallow she made. A gasp broke from her lips, the sound deepening into a moan. He looked up to see Card spreading her thighs and flexing his hips, thrusting into her.

Their gazes locked for long moments before Jayce looked back to Mei's mouth on him. They formed a circuit then, Card pressed into her pussy as Mei took Jayce's cock deep into her mouth, their pleasure a unified strand whipping back and forth through each one of them, echoing and rebounding.

The last time Jayce felt this, it had been the morning before they left for Sareem. He hadn't imagined it would be the last time he came inside her. And thank the goddess it hadn't been.

Her hair draped down over her bare shoulders, tickling the skin of his hips.. Her long, pale lashes swept down over her cheeks as sweet sounds of pleasure echoed up his cock each time she made them.

He didn't want to let go just yet but he'd wanted her so long, loved her so long, it was useless. His hands gripped her shoulders as he came with waves of sensation so intense they intoxicated him.

She pulled away and looked into his eyes. "I love your taste," she murmured.

Mei couldn't shake the incredible sense of connection to Jayce, the feeling of drowning in him and his emotions. His awareness and emotions surrounded her, buffeted her, drew her in and caught her. It was familiar but different and she'd forgotten how much she missed him until she had him back.

And Card—in his raw admission of his origins to Jayce she'd heard the defensiveness and yet Jayce had eased that as she had so many times. She loved them both all the more for how they were to each other as well as her.

She rested her head on Jayce's belly, her hands in his as Card fucked into her body hard and deep. The wide, thick meat of him sliced through her over and over as it had so many times and yet each time it felt even better than it had the last.

Both his hands had been gripping her hips, holding her right where he wanted as he fucked her, but one slid around to her clit, applying just the right amount of pressure over the slick, swollen spot.

"Come for me, Mei," Card murmured.

A cry came from her as orgasm slammed into her body, cunt spasming around his invading cock. She knew he wouldn't be long for it as his thrusts became shallow digs until with a growl of her name he pressed deep and exploded within her.

He pulled out some time later and together with Jayce they pulled her up and settled her between them.

Card listened to her breathing as she fell into sleep. His mind had been racing for the last week with the chase of the darkling and then the threat of nearly losing her. The night hadn't been anything he'd expected it to be but strangely, it was still all right.

In a way, Card had always been threatened by Jayce's memory. He'd never doubted Mei's love and commitment to him but it felt like the memory of her dead first husband was another person in their relationship. How can one compete with a memory?

At first when the memory had been made concrete, panic had raced through his system but at the same time, he knew the Donovan wouldn't have lied. Simply knowing Mei would choose him if asked eased his fears. Seeing her, breathing her in when he'd arrived in Tir na nOg had helped as well. But feeling her bond with Jayce was like a blind spot in his own bond with her. He'd felt unsure of how they'd work things out because there was no way he wanted to share her with any other man, especially one as powerful as Jayce.

The spell had taken the unease and brought contentment. The specter of the memory of Jayce was replaced by something else, a sense of unity, of family. Jayce wasn't the other anymore, he was part of the bond Card had with Mei. There was no threat, only connection.

Chapter Three

ဢ

Jayce woke up and the ache of her memory sliced through him. His hand automatically went to his throat where the ring hung but it was gone. Panicked, he sat up and looked around himself for it only to see her there, eyes wide as she looked at him.

"Jayce? Is everything all right?" Her voice was sleepy as she sat up and traced a fingertip down his jaw. He remembered the ring was on his finger again after three millennia.

"Yes. I just woke up and thought you were gone. I…" He shook his head and she kissed the cleft on his chin.

"But I'm not. I'm here and all the little Fae chickies had better keep that in mind."

He chuckled. "Goddess, I'd forgotten how beautiful you look first thing when you wake." Joy rushed through him as reality replaced the nightmare he'd been living. His woman was back and in his bed. Naked and at his side. Looking up with him with such love and desire it made his chest hurt.

Happiness spread through Mei as she looked into that face that was once as familiar as her own. She wove her hands into his hair and pulled him down to her. "There are other things you seem to have forgotten about me in the morning."

A hand trailed over her from neck to hip. "So soft. Your skin is dusted with silken gold. You're a goddess, Mei. My goddess." He got to his hands and knees, looming over her, his hair sliding over his back and down onto her like a blanket of fire.

Words wouldn't come to her. Oh how she loved him! His muscles, hard and substantial, rippled under her palms as she slid them up his biceps and over his shoulders.

Taking her lips again, he delivered a kiss so dizzying that she briefly wondered if he'd used magic on her. He pulled back and looked deep into her eyes before saying, "I'm going to taste every inch of you, Mei. And after I've done that and listened to your cries as you come, then I'll slide my cock deep inside you and make love to you until we're sated."

Good lord the man was wicked. In all the right ways. It was all she could do to hold back a girlish sigh at his words.

Instead she nodded enthusiastically, like a twenty-year-old. But she wanted him too much to be embarrassed. She wanted his hands and lips on her and right then.

"Your breasts are so beautiful," he murmured just before he closed his mouth over a nipple.

White-hot pleasure shot straight to her pussy. Each draw of his mouth against her nipple created a corresponding throb of her clit.

Her hands smoothed over the muscled flesh of his back and shoulders and then down over the hard flanks of his thighs. Mei had had him just hours before but with Card still deeply sleeping there was something momentous about this moment with this man. It wasn't that they were alone, but in a sense it was just the two of them, reconnecting.

Kissing his way to the other breast, he tasted her nipple, scraping the edge of his teeth across the sensitive tip. His mouth on her was superheated. It was more than him tasting her, it felt as if he was bringing a piece of her into himself.

Down his mouth kissed, over her ribs, tongue flicking over the soft skin there. Pushing her thighs apart, he looked up into her face for a long moment. Using his thumbs, he opened her to his gaze.

"I'd almost forgotten how pretty you are here. Slick and swollen for me. But I do remember your taste. I remember it and want it now."

His words, the cadence and accent in them, held her transfixed until he took a long lick. Her hips bucked and she gasped.

"Sweet. Sweet and a bit salty, like the sea out there."

Her hands found his head, fingers threading through the fiery softness of his hair, holding him to her.

Homecoming. That's what it was as he used one thumb to slowly circle her gate, easing just barely inside, teasing. Her clit hardened under his tongue. He could spend hours there, tasting her, finding his way through every fold and dip. He feasted on her body and her fevered response to him. So soft and wet.

Her clit was a plump berry against his tongue. He drew the edge of his teeth across it as he slipped two fingers up into her cunt. The way she clutched at him made his cock throb against the mattress beneath him, aching to be inside her.

But right then he wanted to make her come, and judging by the way she writhed beneath him, making soft sounds of need and desire, she wanted that too.

Sucking her clit in between his lips, the tip of his tongue flicked it quick and featherlight as he hooked his fingers, stroking them over her sweet spot. Her body tightened and she cried out as she began to come.

Orgasm slammed into Mei's body and there was nothing else but Jayce's mouth against her, his fingers deep inside her. Wave after wave of pleasure buffeted her in an unyielding grip. Back bowed, muscles taut, she held his head to her as his name came from her lips in a hoarse whisper.

Her muscles were still twitching through the aftereffects of climax when he moved up her body and kissed her softly on each closed eyelid.

"Mei, ride me. I want to see you rise above me like the golden goddess you are." He rolled, bringing her with him, and she sat up, thighs astride his.

Rising up, she reached back and guided him true. "This is like a dream." She hovered there, the head of him just inside her.

"No, it's real. Thank the heavens above. It's real and you're alive. And right now I just want to fuck you. We can work out the rest later."

She might have said something, touched by his words, but the flex of his hips brought the full length of his cock into her and she was powerless to do more than arch her back at the arc of electric pleasure that came from the way he felt filling her up so completely.

His hands came to her hips, palms flat, holding her still. Their eyes locked and Mei felt as if she'd fallen into his gaze. Felt like he saw straight into her heart in a way that was special to him. Having that connection with him again made her heart pound and her blood heat. Fear mixed with desire. She'd had it and lost it. She didn't think she could bear to lose it again.

"Ride, *a thaisce*, ride."

His treasure. It'd been three thousand years since she'd heard the endearment from him. Three millennia since she'd heard the Gaelic from his lips with the touch of Fae tingeing the accent.

"You feel so good around me, Mei."

Looking down at him she smiled, it was impossible not to. His hair was spread about him like a wild river, eyes of an otherworldly amethyst-blue stared up at her. Stared *into* her.

His cock sliced through her over and over as she rose up and slammed herself down onto him. A swivel created a mashing friction of her clit against his pelvic bone. Drawing her fingertips up each rib and tracing circles around his nipples, she watched his lips part, his breathing quicken.

Her breasts swayed with her rhythm on him and he cupped their weight, flicking his thumbs over her nipples.

One of his hands strayed down, finding her clit and squeezing it gently between his thumb and forefinger.

A surprised gasp burst from her lips and he felt her pussy begin to squeeze and flutter around him as her orgasm hit her.

Joy at making her feel so good and the way he felt so deep inside her pushed him over. Grabbing her hips, he held her to him as he thrust up into her and came.

In that moment he gave her everything, his heart, his soul, his belief that she was meant to be his as he was inextricably hers.

She slumped over, her head on his chest as their breath slowed to normal. Idly, he stroked a fingertip down her spine.

"I love you, Jayce," she murmured against his skin.

"And I you. I do think I feel fortified for what will definitely be a challenging day."

In the background, Card began to stir as he sat up. "My, whatever did I miss?"

* * * * *

The three of them, all holding hands, entered Aine's private chambers. She was there and working already and looked up as they came in.

"Darling." Smiling, she stood and went to Mei, embracing her and kissing both cheeks. "You look well. Much better than when I left you last evening. Carl visited me and told me of the spell." She turned to Card. "I understand you're my son-in-law. Welcome to Tir na nOg and thank you for saving my child." She kissed his cheeks and Mei wanted to laugh as he blushed.

"It's an honor to meet you, your majesty. I'm so relieved that Mei can come back home and things weren't what they seemed."

Aine cocked her head. "Thank you for that, Card. That means much to me. Carl told me how you were instrumental in saving Mei from Carthau. He also said your love and support are what got Mei through the time when...after she'd thought we'd exiled her." Aine's voice cracked with emotion.

Mei moved to her mother. "I forgive you. It wasn't your fault. You didn't know. Please don't take this on yourself."

"He told me it took nearly three hundred years for the wounds on your wrists to heal! He told me there was so much internal damage Freya had to petition the council to have healing performed by The Bona Dea. Even for her it was a challenge."

Jayce sucked in his breath and turned to Mei.

"He shouldn't have told you that. He had no right to tell you."

Card pulled Mei to his side and she breathed him in, needed that comfort.

"No, he shouldn't have told her. You should have. Mei, how could you not tell me? I'm your mate, your husband. Card helped you shoulder that burden, why not me?"

"Don't make this about yourself, Jayce. I was there, yes. It wasn't pretty and she woke up screaming for hundreds of years. But it's passed. When should she have told you? When she agreed to be bound to us both? In bed between us after we'd shared love and sighs? It's her story, let her tell it, or not, as she needs to." Card's voice was calm and deep, the bass of it vibrated through her and she felt better, reassured.

"He's right. I'm sorry. I am making it about me. I feel like I failed you and another man didn't and that's my problem and not yours, Mei. I do want you to share with me but at your own pace. Please though, I do want you to know I want to help shoulder part of that in whatever way I can." Jayce reached out and touched her face, bringing a thumb along her jawline.

"Darling, Carl just answered my questions. I'm your mother, I had to know and he told me when I asked. I'm sorry to have upset you."

"Let's just move on, shall we?" Mei asked, sitting down at the table and drinking some tea. "I'm hungry and I'd like to know if the truthseeker has arrived."

Card joined her on one side and Aine sat across from them and they all began to eat as the tension ebbed away.

"I will speak with my people to see what's happened. I'll return momentarily." Jayce kissed the top of Mei's head and she squeezed his hand.

"I love you."

He knelt beside her and she ran a hand through his hair. "I love you too, Mei. Goddess, I'm so glad to have you back."

Mei smiled. "I'm glad too."

Jayce left the room for several minutes as Aine got to know Card. Or rather, interrogated him in her own indomitable way. For a demon he was very easygoing most of the time and took it with good nature.

Just as Jayce came back to fill them in, Aine got to the real point.

"If you don't mind my asking, and please don't think I'm rude, because I love that you love my daughter and saved her and you're her husband and —"

"But how did a woman who was tortured for a thousand years in a demon prison end up with a man who is half demon?" Card interrupted.

"Yes."

But it was Mei who spoke, an edge in her voice. "When Card found me I was very close to death. I wanted to die many times. I'd willed it but Xethan, the warden, had warded my cell and the cuffs so I couldn't use any magic and only demon magic would work. It was his magic that kept me alive even when I should have died. Many times over.

"Only a demon or someone using demon magic could help me. Donovan sent Card, who'd joined the warriors about five hundred years before. When he came to me, he'd killed his way through three levels. He saved me." Mei shrugged and caressed Card's thigh.

"I never thought of him as one of them. He isn't. He proved that to me the very first moment I saw him. That's all there is to it." Mei sent her mother a look that made it clear there was to be no further discussion of the issue.

"The truthseeker is on his way. They're under guard. Cullen is in charge. We will get our answers." Jayce sat next to Mei.

There was a tap on the door and Aine waved Jayce to stay seated as she called for whoever it was to enter.

Jayce and Mei both stood, ready for battle. "Mother! You can't just do that. You have guards here for that. You don't know who it is."

"It's me!" Conchobar rushed into the room and stopped, stunned when he caught sight of Mei. "No! They said you…" He looked to Jayce, who nodded. "Oh, sunshine, this is good news to salve the bad."

"Bad? What is it?" Aine snapped to attention and a tall, dark-haired woman rushed into the room, eyes red and frantic.

"They took Elise!"

"Who? Who took her?" Jayce moved forward, his arm around Mei's waist. The dark-haired woman looked at Mei, puzzled.

"Dark Fae. They sent this note." The woman thrust it at Jayce, who took it. Mei and Card looked over his shoulder to read it as well.

"Fuckety fuck! They want Eire freed or they'll harm the babe." Mei sighed explosively.

"Who are you?"

Mei looked up and took the other woman's hands. "I'm Mei. Aine's daughter. You must be Em."

Jayce put his hand up. "There's *so* much you need to know, but for now let's deal with this."

"They want to meet face-to-face to give their specific demands. I'll go." Mei waved a hand and was changed into jeans, boots and a long-sleeved shirt. Her hair was back in a ponytail.

"You will not!" Aine and Jayce said at once.

"I will. Look, Mother, you can't very well go off and meet with some lowly Dark Fae. It's totally unsafe!" She turned to Jayce. "And you, you're her first-in-command, you need to be here, keeping her safe and dealing with the blowback from this. Card can't go because he's not Fae. I am the logical choice."

"Sunshine, I appreciate your wanting to help but a warrior needs to do this." Con tried to sound reasonable.

Mei growled and showed him the magical brand at the inside of her wrist. "I am a warrior for the Balance. I have been for nearly two thousand years. I survived a thousand years in Carthau, I am most certainly able to handle anything the Dark Fae throw at me. And if you recall, you trained me as a Favored guard. I'm not helpless."

"A *thousand* years in Carthau?" Con's voice nearly broke.

Mei paused and looked back to Em. "You're her mother. You don't know me at all but I can tell you that your child means something to me and I'll tell you why after she's back in your arms again. I will not do anything to harm her. I swear to you on my own life."

Em nodded. "I believe you. I can feel your sincerity. But you love my husband. Why is that and does Jayce know? And this one too?" Em motioned at Card. "You're a busy Fae."

Con started, looking at Mei, surprised, and Jayce chuckled.

"Ah, you're an empath?" Mei asked Em.

58

"Yes."

"Well. I'd prefer it if we could have done this better but we don't have that luxury now. Em, I hate to say it this way but we don't have a lot of time and I want you to know why I love your husband. He's my brother. Elise is my niece and you're my sister-in-law."

"What?" Con's voice thundered through the room as he rounded on Aine.

"She's telling the truth. Your father and I... Well, you know that he and I were together before your mother came along and I botched it. Badly. It was only once, who knew I'd get pregnant? He felt guilty and I didn't want to break up his family and his marriage and so I lied and told him Mei wasn't his. It's a long story, let's get Elise taken care of and we'll talk. I promise."

Con turned and looked at Mei, who'd gotten very still, waiting to see how he'd react. He took one step and then another and suddenly she was in his arms. "Go. Go and get my daughter. Please," he said into her hair.

She looked around him at Em, who nodded, tears in her eyes.

"They want to meet in the middle of the Square. On the benches that surround the reflecting pool. I'll walk there instead of shimmering. I want the element of surprise."

"Mei, please be careful. I can't bear to lose you again right after you've been restored to me." Aine pressed a kiss to her forehead.

Jayce spun her and kissed her hard, on the lips. Breaking the kiss, he narrowed his eyes. "What your mother said. I'm sending some of my men to shadow you. They'll glamour away the braids and long hair that identify them as Favored. I will hear no argument."

"You'll get none. I'll be back as soon as I can."

Card held his arms out to her and she went to him. "You sure this isn't a situation where I can get your back? I don't like leaving you out in the open like this."

She shook her head. "I need you here. If there's cleanup to be done, do it. I truly don't think this is going to end badly out there. They need Eire and if they attempt to harm me they won't get her. And let's not leave out the fact that I'm a bad ass muthafucka." She winked and he laughed.

"I adore you." He kissed her softly and she hugged him, standing back.

"Me too."

Mei turned and walked out of Aine's private entrance. She exited the palace through the gardens and centered herself on the short walk to the Square.

She saw the man standing at the reflecting pool. He looked nervous. As well he should. Mei planned to wipe the floor with him when this was all over.

She sent out her magic as she approached. There was one other Dark Fae on a bench across the pool but no others. They probably couldn't risk being uncovered. Either that or they didn't have the numbers. Mei suspected it was the former instead of the latter.

"Talk before I slit your throat." Without ceremony she flopped onto the bench and crossed her legs, her ankle over her knee. It also made the knife in her boot closer.

"Who are you?" He rounded on her with a sneer.

"I am Mei NiaAine, princess and next-in-line. *You* are on borrowed time. So talk."

"She is…you are…"

Mei snorted. "Why did they send a mental weakling to do this? I am not dead. You are here because someone with more brains than you snatched a baby to use her as leverage to get Eire back. Eire, my aunt? The one who's in a holding room with a truthseeker on the way? Ringing any bells?"

The other Fae walked around and shoved the first one to the side. "Excuse him. I am Lorcan. What we want is simple. You give us Eire, we give you the babe."

"And I can trust you because you're so trustworthy and all."

"My. A thousand years in a demon prison have made you jaded."

"Ahhh, there we go. Someone with their finger on the pulse. Okay, so here's the thing, I can't trust you. You're a liar and you run with liars. My aunt is queen of the liars, which sadly for her will be the only kind of queen she'll ever be."

"Mei…"

"I have not given you permission to be familiar. You may refer to me as princess or next-in-line."

A slight incline of the head from Lorcan satisfied Mei for the moment.

"Princess, I make no bones about the fact that it is our goal to drive your mother from the throne and install Eire on it in her stead. I can give you the five-minute introduction to Dark Fae party politics but it seems to me that you must be familiar with them on some level."

"You hate humans, blah blah blah. You think we should crush them, yadda yadda. Got it. You're not a bunch of special snowflakes you know. It's such a common agenda that they should sell the boilerplate contracts at Office Depot. Just insert some supposed superior group in slot A and the supposed inferior group in slot B."

"You've been on Earth a lot, I see." He sneered.

"Hmm, enough for you to know what I'm talking about so don't pretend you aren't all eating corn dogs and watching *Laguna Beach* okay, Lorcan? So back to your agenda, cue *duh duh duh* music here. I'm trembling with the awesomeness of your plan. But we were talking about how I can trust you to give me the babe alive and unharmed if we give you Eire."

"We will give the babe to a third party to deliver to the palace unharmed if you do a blood oath that you'll release Eire in exchange."

"I'll be back. I need to run this by the queen."

Lorcan grabbed her arm. "Don't even think about sending troops out here. If we are taken the child will die. If the truthseeker even so much as speaks in Eire's direction she will die."

Mei saw the light of a zealot in his eyes. Shaking free, she said, "If we were planning to kill you *at this moment,* you'd be dead. Now unhand me. You have no leave to touch me. You are beneath contempt. I give you my word. I stand by my word. I will return with your answer and no one will attempt to capture you before we either give you Eire or send you packing. My word is my bond, you need no blood spell from me. After this is over, however, I will hunt you down and separate you from your life."

Without another word she shimmered into the garden near the back entrance and walked back through to her mother's rooms.

"They'll do it," Mei said bluntly. "The Fae I just met with, Lorcan, is from an old family. He doesn't seem to realize I know who he is and where he comes from. But he's a zealot and he has a cause. He'll kill Elise if we don't give them Eire. They don't care. They have an agenda and they have nothing to lose. If the truthseeker gets to Eire before they do their whole plan will be exposed."

"You can't be thinking of giving in! Mei, she told me you were dead! She let you rot in Carthau for a thousand years. She sent you away, leaving you to believe I'd abandoned you. She's been a traitor to her people!" Aine stood and began to pace.

"I'm not arguing with what Eire is and what she's done. When the time comes you can believe she will absolutely pay the price and no one will stop me. But Elise is an innocent child. Em is a mother like you were a mother. We cannot let this baby be harmed. I cannot! We would get information from a truthseeker, yes, but at what price, Mother? Haven't enough daughters been taken from their mothers?"

"If we don't get the truth from her how many millions will die? All innocents?" asked Cullen, Jayce's cousin who was one of the Favored in the room.

Card watched it all before speaking. "We know the key points. We know about the rifts. We know the Dark Fae are involved. We do not need the blood of innocent children on our hands to handle this."

Mei smiled at him briefly for backing her up. "We will find out the truth. I swear on it. But we can get answers without this baby having to die. I won't stop until we eradicate the threat of the Dark Fae. And we have Brian. They haven't asked about him and I wonder if they know he's been taken too. Let's get that truthseeker in to Brian as soon as he arrives here."

She told them about the plans to deliver Elise if Mei took a blood oath to give them Eire.

"Please. Oh please, Aine! I've rarely asked you for anything but I'm begging you now, please let Mei save my baby's life," Em asked through tears.

"Aine, majesty, please," Con echoed his wife quietly.

"Jayce? What think you of this?" Aine looked to him.

"We could have the truthseeker go directly to Brian and begin with him as we bring Eire out. Grab Elise before Eire can tell them we have Brian. That's the only way I can see this working."

They agreed to do it that way and Mei shimmered directly there this time and relayed the agreement. She also patently refused a blood oath.

"Take it or leave it. My word is my word. I have lived with honor and if I tell you I'm going to do something I'll do it."

Lorcan looked her up and down and nodded shortly. "I will have the child brought to the side gates in five minutes. Bring Eire then."

She shimmered back and they made plans to move Eire.

"There is a spell I learned from some old associates of mine. It slows thought and speech. I believe we should perform this spell on Eire so she is unable to speak right away. It is nearly undetectable and it'll wear off in a short period, probably before she even realizes she's been bespelled. It'll give us a bit more time to get Elise before Eire says anything about Brian."

"Do it." Aine waved her acceptance.

As magic wouldn't work in the holding rooms, Mei put the magic cuffs on her aunt and bespelled her on the walk toward the audience chamber. The truthseeker had been rushed and was entering the holding area as they left.

"What do you want?" Eire asked belligerently.

"Your compatriots have stolen an infant to ransom you. Such noble behavior for those who claim to be the best our race has to offer. You must be proud."

"I knew they wouldn't let you harm me."

Eire's nonchalance at hearing a child had been ransomed for her made Mei want to throttle her. Instead she gave a feral smile and as the guards moved things around and got Eire ready, she performed the spell.

Mei knew it had worked when Eire's eyes got blurry a moment and then cleared. She leaned in, grabbing her aunt's hair and holding her still while she spoke in her ear. "I just want you to know that I'm coming for you, Eire.. You may have won this time but you can't run from me forever. You owe me. I *will* collect."

Mei let go as Eire started to complain and led the way down the hall to the gate.

Con stood at the gate and waited, his face impassive. Em was back with Aine. Card was in the background somewhere,

Mei felt his presence and knew if anyone made a false move he'd be on them in a moment.

Mei stopped and turned to Eire. "Wait here, you treacherous bitch. I'm going to get that child and then you can enjoy your last days."

Con nodded at Mei and grabbed Eire's upper arm, holding her there. The cuffs would ensure she was unable to sift or shimmer.

At the gate a guard stood, holding a chubby dark-haired child that Mei guessed was her niece. Without turning around she called out to Con, "Is that her?"

"Yes."

Mei admired the steel in his voice. "I'm going to get her and shimmer her to safety, Con. I'll see you in a few moments."

She approached and kept her eye open for traps.. Theoretically, in the palace no dark magic could be done but who knew what Eire had done. "I'll take the babe." She reached out and with a laugh, Elise came into her arms, taking Mei's face between her hands and giving a gummy smile.

"They handed her to me. Told me you'd know what to do." The guard looked a bit bewildered.

For a moment Mei thought about keeping Eire but she'd given her word and that was the kind of old magic that would rebound. Turning to look back at Con once more, she shimmered into her mother's apartments as he removed the cuffs.

"Momma!" Elise clapped when she saw Em.

With a gasp, Em ran to them and pulled her daughter to her, kissing the upturned face.

Aine went to Mei and hugged her tight, relieved. Jayce was with Brian and the truthseeker and Con shimmered into the room and moved to bring his wife and child into his arms.

Card entered shortly thereafter and moved to Mei's side. They'd worked together in dangerous situations for two thousand years and she appreciated the feeling of ease and the confidence he had in her abilities.

When Jayce came in with a long face he immediately sought out Mei, making sure she was still there.

"It's bad." He sat down on a chaise and Mei took his hand. "They've amassed an army. They've been rifting to other worlds for the last two thousand years, most seriously in the last five years. Eire was to be their queen. Getting rid of Mei was a way to keep her from the throne and keep Aine weakened. Eire wanted to kill Mei right off but there was a powerful magic keeping Mei alive. Brian didn't know what it was and neither did Eire but that's why they sent her away instead of killing her.

"They know the rifting is dangerous and unstable. They don't care. If they go, they'll take everyone else with them. He gave the names of other Dark Fae here in the palace. I sent men to arrest them. Most of them had gone but those who stayed are in holding now. The truthseeker has sent for others who can help him."

Aine's secretary came in. "Majesty, I'm sorry to disturb you but there's a crowd gathering. People have heard rumors, they want to know what's going on."

"In ten minutes we'll be out." Aine stood and brushed her palms down her gown. She looked at the three of them on the chaise. "They've declared war."

"Yes, Aine, they have."

"And we'll have to declare it right back." Mei stood.

Jayce took her hand. "Yes."

"When the Audience is over, I'd love to visit with you for a while. I've always wanted a sister." Con grinned. "And I've missed you, sunshine. Come and see us, play with Elise, get to know Em."

Em kissed Mei's cheeks. "Thank you. You saved her."

Mei shrugged. "She's my niece. The price wasn't worth it. We can get the information another way."

* * * * *

Mei watched her mother in awe. She handled the anxious crowd well, reassuring them that the Dark Fae would be taken out and advising them all to be watchful and careful.

The Favored would be hyper-vigilant now all over Tir na nOg. They'd report to Con on any information they found regarding the rifts. The Favored were larger than most Fae knew, keeping well trained but staying quiet most of the time, living their lives until needed. That moment was now and they'd all report in and be assigned.

Afterward they went back to their quarters and Jayce, Card and Mei shimmered to Con and Em's home in Tir na nOg.

"Come on in and have a seat. I've just gotten Elise down for a nap. She looks no worse for wear. Her mental and emotional states are all right. Thank goodness they didn't harm her." Em met them at the door and waved them inside.

"This is Card Leviathan, he's my mate as well." Mei introduced Card to Con and Em.

"Well that's new." Con looked to Jayce. "And how do you feel about that?"

Mei started to speak but Card put a hand on her shoulder and shook his head.

"Card saved her from Carthau. He's been at her side for the last two thousand years. He loves her and she loves him. Without him she'd be dead or still there. Would I prefer that to having her here? I don't know, Conchobar, what would you think in my position?" Jayce challenged.

He explained the binding spell Freya performed. "We are all bound to each other. I love Card as I love Mei. Well, not quite the same way." He chuckled. "But he is the brother of my heart. And I owe him everything for bringing her back to me."

Con turned to Card and bowed his head a moment. "I apologize if I've made you feel unwelcome. Jayce is as a brother to me, I do not wish any unhappiness for him. Please, be welcome to my home."

Card took the hand Con held out, shaking it.

"You're not done," Em said to Con.

"What?"

"Your sister. You've invited her here and cut off her mate to her face. You've asked Jayce how he felt and you've apologized to Card. But you've said nothing to Mei."

Con turned to Mei, who had her arms crossed over her chest.

Card shook his head. "It's all right. He wanted to protect his friend. I'm not upset and it's no less than I would do in his place. I expect Jayce will get much the same treatment among the warriors and in my pack."

"This is between Con and me. Walk with me," Mei called over her shoulder as she went back outside.

"Well, get to it. I'll prepare a meal and these two handsome specimens can help me." Em winked at Jayce and Card before looking back at Con. "Go on then. She's your sister. Believe me, I know what that's like."

Con sighed and followed Mei out, finding her sitting on one of the sand dunes near the house. He sat next to her. "I'm sorry if I wasn't welcoming. I can't apologize that my first concern was for Jayce."

"I introduced my husband as I entered your home. You had no right to not even speak to him. And don't bother apologizing in one breath and telling me you don't apologize in the next."

Con laughed and put his arm around her shoulders. "I have missed you. I must admit you're a bit harder-edged than you used to be. I imagine a thousand years in a place like Carthau might harden you a bit."

"A bit."

"What I am sorry for is hurting your feelings. I loved you before I knew you were my sister, you know.. I mourned your loss and I watched Jayce ache for a thousand years. I'm glad you're back and alive and I'm glad of it in part because Jayce is whole again. If I said I was sorry for checking in with Jayce first before welcoming Card I'd be lying. I try not to do that. I didn't cut him to hurt you. I made Jayce my priority. I'm glad the three of you have made it work. I truly am. And I'm glad as hell and heaven that you are restored."

"Card was there for me when no one else was. He's accepted this with such courage and tenacity. He puts me first always, even when it hurts him. I will not, ever, have him disrespected. He is better than most everyone I've ever met and he's had to deal with a lot being what he is. I won't have it. I won't, Conchobar MacNessa. He is my husband. My mate. And he is my life. If anyone had treated Em that way, how would you have felt?"

Con sighed. "I understand. I'm sorry and I make you my solemn promise that I'll show him and you the respect he deserves. We okay?"

"Yes. Em is gorgeous and Elise is beautiful. I'd love to go and see Finn. I understand he's got a wife and twin boys."

Con's face warmed at the mention of Em and his daughter. "Em is gorgeous, inside and out. Ten thousand years I waited. She was worth every moment. And Elise? A greater joy in the world than hearing that sweet voice call out for her Da I've yet to experience.

"As for Finn? He'll be as happy as I am with the news. He married Magda NiaMaeve and yes, they have boys. They'll keep you on your toes."

"Magda? Her mother is the teacher at the language school? Pretty, big blue eyes?"

Con laughed. "Yes, that's her and yes, she's still teaching. The boys have her look about them. Which is a relief because Finn's ugly mug shouldn't be reproduced."

Mei laughed and punched his shoulder playfully. "Go on with you. Your brother Finn has quite a pleasing face!"

"Your brother too. I still can't quite get over it. Da would have been so glad of it, you know. He would have done right by you. I'm sorry beyond words that you spent all those years thinking you were alone."

"I wasn't alone. I had Card. But Eire will pay. Con, I'm not sure you should tell your mother. I don't want her to be hurt. What my mother did was wrong. What our father did was wrong. And I don't think it's a positive to anyone to say anything now."

"I know one thing and it's that our father would not want your origins hidden. It shouldn't be on you."

"Oh," she flapped a hand, "please. Conchobar, you know as well as I do that it's not a big deal. I'm five thousand years old and it hasn't exactly hurt me. I'm next in line to the throne."

"Hurt you?" He stood up and began to stomp back to the house where Card and Jayce waited on the porch. Card began to move but Jayce put a hand out to stop him.

"Hurt you? A thousand years in a demon prison sounds like you were hurt!" he called back over his shoulder.

"That wasn't because my father cheated on his wife for one afternoon five thousand years ago, Conchobar! That was because my aunt is crazy and power mad. That's Dark Fae, not our father and my mother's stupidity. And don't you stomp off." She hurried after him.

"You suffered all this time and I didn't know! I would have helped you, damn it. You would not have suffered for millennia if I'd known you were alive."

"What is it with you all? You don't get to make this about you. I served those damned thousand years. They're mine. My millstone. You don't get to wrap yourself in guilt for not knowing something you couldn't have known. So shut up. We're not telling your mother and that's final. No one else knows but Finn. I say so and that's that."

She breezed by him and went into the house, where Em handed her a glass of juice.

"She's an even bigger pain in the ass now," Con grumbled when he reached the front porch.

Em looked at Mei and laughed.

"She is, but goddess she's magnificent when she does it," Jayce said as he followed Mei into the house.

"My manners were less than they should have been for my brother-in-law." Con looked to Card. "I apologize."

Card shrugged. "As I said, I'm sure Jayce might just face much the same from my people. It's all right. I respect loyalty. Just so you understand Mei is my wife. I will be at her side where she goes. Period."

"I like that. Good." Con nodded and they all sat down.

"Okay, now that feathers have been ruffled and everyone knows their place, perhaps we can get down to saving the world?" Mei said.

Jayce filled them in on the situation and Mei explained about the rifts.

"Sounds like some tracking is in order then. Em, if we're here, we'll be staying in the palace. This home isn't as safe as I'd like. If you're in New Orleans I want you at Lee's or Holly's. Jayce, I'll work with Cullen on the tracking."

"I'm the best you'll ever find," Card spoke.

"He's right. Card is the best tracker I've ever seen. He's been my partner for nearly two thousand years. We've tracked a lot of nasty over that time. I'll get on the intelligence gathering. We need to know what their plan is."

"I can't believe you think you can just order me off like some kind of pet! Conchobar MacNessa, I will be a part of this if I think I should," Em huffed indignantly.

Mei hid a smile at the exchange but Jayce didn't bother.

"Lucky for you, mister, I think it's a good idea. I have every intention of having Elise in the safest possible place." Em smirked.

"You're a test, Emily Charvez. A test on my poor heart and constitution."

Mei burst out laughing.

"However," Em said and Con groaned. "I happen to know a tad about magic. Remember?"

"We may need it. Opening a rift is one thing, difficult but doable with the right kind of magic and set of gifts. Not many Fae can do it but it's possible according to the history texts. But completely closing one is far more complicated. It's why the leaks of matter are such a problem.." Mei pursed her lips as she thought.

"Okay, I can start the research. Can you do it? Open and close a rift?" Em asked Mei.

"I don't know. Supposedly my maternal line carries the gift of opening rifts. It's like tearing a piece of paper. I think I can deal with that theoretically. But I don't know if I can close one. And closing it well enough to stop the matter leak, I suppose we'll have to see. Jayce?" Mei turned to him.

"I can't even open one. You make it sound easy. Don't underestimate the power you have, Mei."

Mei blushed and Card snorted. "She does it all the time. Minimizes her power, her gifts."

"Okay, okay. Moving along. My mother might have the power. She's strong and gifted. It's just not something the Fae have done in probably fifteen, more like thirty thousand years. There are texts in her library about the troll wars. Rifting was something they did, caused a lot of damage with."

"She's given me access to her library. Perhaps Elise and I will set up camp in there for a bit. Goodness knows it's warded up tight."

Con narrowed his eyes, readying for a battle, but growled and shook his head. "If she re-wards it to keep Eire out, it's acceptable for you to be there. Safe."

Chapter Four

ဢ

Lorcan paced the wide rooms of the palatial residence in Sh'mura. "I can't believe that bitch had Brian too! Why didn't you say something?"

"I did when I got to you." Eire pouted prettily.

"Too little too late. Now they know who our people are in the palace who didn't get out."

"She's the first one against the wall when I take the throne. Self-righteous, uptight bitch. Imagine the audacity to hold *me* prisoner! You're the one who should have made her take a blood oath." Eire sat down with a pout.

"She is many things, honorable most of all. She did not break her promise to you. Unlike you and yours, she kept her word. She brought you as promised. It was you who underestimated her. I did once as well. You're lucky she didn't kill you. I would have. Come to think of it, that would have saved us a lot of trouble. She's not given to a lot of emotionalism so the choice must not have been hers."

Eire turned her gaze to Xethan, narrowing one of her eyes. "I don't like how you speak to me."

"Hmm, I think I'll cry a thousand salty tears."

Lorcan laughed and stopped himself when Eire looked in his direction.

"Why is he speaking this way to me? I'm your queen!"

Lorcan sighed heavily. "Everyone needs to calm down. We need to move to the next step."

"As long as you remember that Mei is mine. No one harms her. She is to be delivered to me. That is your price for my help. If she is damaged or killed, my wrath will be great."

Lorcan tried not to wince at Xethan's words, but nodded.

* * * * *

Mei stood in the meadow, watching Card. He'd shifted into wolf form, scenting the grass, the flowers, the very air. Shifter magic painted the area as he assumed a humanoid form again, quickly pulling on pants, staying shirtless. A shiver broke over her as she watched the muscles of his upper body play and flex as he stalked over to them. Their gazes caught and held for long moments and a brief, knowing smile broke over his lips before he turned his attentions to the group.

"Four Fae worked the spell. Dark magic. The same as at the other site. Where they're rifting to I don't know but the magic feels the same. At least a dozen Fae, probably more, were in this meadow. Not longer than two days ago."

"I can see the energy leaking." They'd used magic to define the edges so it was visible to the naked eye.

"Can you stop it?" Card walked around the rift.

"I don't know."

Jayce ordered everyone to move back and Mei knelt near the rift site, feeling the cool trickle of the matter leaking through. Reaching inside herself, she grabbed the spark of her magic, tended it until it glowed and let it flow through her.

She visualized herself knitting the edges of the rift, pulling the universe back together and making it whole. For a moment she felt her magic reach out like two hands and pull the fabric back together. But it slipped from her grasp until she lost it completely and came back to herself again.

Twilight had fallen, pink and cool, about the Fae gathered in the meadow, watching.

"Wow. How long was I working?"

Card helped her to stand, her muscles tight after kneeling for so long. The warmth seeped through his palms as he kneaded her calves.

"About three hours. It's not totally closed but it's better than it was," Card said as he stood and kissed her forehead.

"You did a great job, *a thaisce*." Jayce pulled her to him briefly. "Did you learn anything?"

"There's something familiar about the magic on the other side of the rift. Could you taste it, Card?"

"I couldn't sense anything on the other side. The matter flowing through had no taste at all. What I sensed was all here on this side.."

"The truthseekers spent the day with the other Dark Fae we captured back at the palace. Let's go back and talk to them and see what they found. And see if Em came up with anything. And I want you to eat and rest. You must be tired." Jayce held his hand out and she took it. "I'm leaving sentries here, just remote sentry spells but it should be enough to alert us if anyone uses any magic here."

They shimmered back to the gardens outside the palace and walked back through. Mei magicked herself out of her work clothes and into a gown she knew her mother would expect.

The wards had been tightened so that no one could shimmer in or out of the inner walls. Eire's magical signature was banned and within the personal apartments only Aine, Mei, Card, Jayce and a few others were allowed their magic. The truthseeker had interviewed all the Favored, at their own request, to be sure Aine and Mei were safe.

Aine stood as they all entered. "Well?"

Mei shook her head. "I made it better but I couldn't fix it. The magic kept falling from my grasp. It was... I don't know how to describe it. Slippery? Slick? I couldn't figure it out."

Aine went to her and held Mei's face between her palms. "Darling, don't feel bad. I doubt many alive could have done as much as you did. Rift magic is old. So very old. It's not a gift you see much anymore. It's rather a shame that the Dark Fae decided to squander it for an unjust cause. If they had come to me, this gift could've been used for good and not ill. Whoever it is, clearly they've got a lot of power."

"Majesty, perhaps you can go and look at it? Mei says it's a gift that runs in her maternal line." Jayce bowed his head a moment.

"Truth be told, I've never done it. My mother could. I remember being told a story about it when I was very young. She used it during the troll wars. Perhaps this may also run in Nessa's line. His is old as well."

"I tried it, Aine, I couldn't make heads or tails of it. I couldn't even see the energy leak through the rift until Mei pointed it out." Con stood forward.

"All right then. Mei, you will eat and rest. Do not argue with me. I will take Jayce and Con and a retinue of guards to the site, see what I can see."

"Mother, I'm a warrior, I can protect you."

"I'm sure you can. But so can they." Aine waved at the column of warriors in front of her. "Now go. I'm queen, one of the best parts of the job is that you all have to obey me." One of her eyebrows rose and Card chuckled.

"Now I know where you get it," he murmured.

"Fine. But I want you back here within an hour. And I want someone to come to me right away when you return. If you're not back in an hour I'm coming to find you and then I'll be cranky, Mother."

Aine laughed and kissed Mei's cheeks. "Now go. Card, you be sure she eats and puts her feet up."

Card nodded. Jayce moved to her and kissed her lips. "Listen to them both. I'll be back soon and if you haven't rested I'm going to spank you."

"Promise?"

His grin was wicked and gooseflesh rose on Mei's arms.

"Oh it's that way, is it? Hmm, well, I always like new things and your ass is delectable," he whispered in her ear. "Now go. I'm sure Card has a few ideas on how to get you warmed up. *After* you eat."

They left as she watched and Card took her hand as they went to their rooms.

* * * * *

Once inside their suite Mei found herself backed to the wall, Card's big body caging her. "I've wanted to touch you for hours," he murmured before his lips took hers.

"Card—" She began to speak but he tsked.

"Mei, stop it. I want you. I want you all the time. I wanted you as the power glowed from you in the meadow. I promise to feed you grapes and wine when I'm finished. I'll have to because you'll be much too tired for anything else. And then you'll rest for real." He ground his cock into her belly. His fingertips brushed up the inside of her thigh as he pushed her gown out of the way. Sliding his fingers over her pussy, he exhaled softly. "And I see you want me too. So let's stop arguing until after I've had you a few times."

"You always did have the best ideas...ohhhh." She gasped as he dropped to his knees and shoved the gown out of the way and buried his face in her pussy. The door was cool against her back, keeping her in contact with reality even as his mouth began to devastate her.

From the first time he'd touched her, even as she'd been nearly dead from what they'd done to her at Carthau, her spirit had responded to his. At first it was just a spark, but it had been there. And then the first time he'd made love to her, slow and gentle even as she knew he'd wanted to take her hard and fast, there'd been no doubt she was made for him. She burned for his touch, woke with thoughts of him, dreamed of him. He'd taken her in every way imaginable in every place they'd been and yet she never got enough.

He'd told her he loved her from the first moment he watched her twist the neck of one of her guards and step over him like so much garbage. He'd said her will to live and survive shone from her. She knew most thought him cold, emotionless. But with her he was gentle and rough, hard and soft, always loving and caring. Her needs were paramount. He'd told her the night he'd proposed that her very existence had saved him from a life marked by one violent episode to the next. He'd not only pledged his love to her but his life. Even with his mouth on her, hot tongue sliding through her pussy, the words echoed through her mind.

He pulled his face back. "You're thinking about something other than me eating your pussy. This vexes me."

Suddenly she stood there, breeze cool against her skin. They were both naked. His magic was just as strong as Fae magic. The man had the moves, no doubt about it.

"Now, Mei, you will stop thinking of ways to resist me. Right this moment. Because it is impossible. I am your mate. Such things are fated and Fate would not deign to hear your arguments even if she didn't kill you for trying. Fate is testy sometimes and has a cracked sense of humor, obviously."

"I wouldn't dream of resisting you, Card Leviathan. I'm all yours."

With a grin, he stood, taking her wrists and bringing them above her head. "Well, that's what a man likes to hear. Hold on to the top of the door." He moved back, looked her up and down with wicked intent and then nodded. "It's time to get with my program of lots of sex and orgasms. You'll need the serotonin rush from climax to stimulate the nerves in your brain."

"Thank you, Mr. Science." The impact of her snarky comeback was diminished when her voice came out as a whispered purr.

He smiled down at her like a predator, his body crowding against hers, caging her. Leaning in, he left an openmouthed kiss at the base of her throat and she broke out in shivers from the heat of his mouth.

Hands braced on either side of her head, he chuckled and whipped his head and moved his body so his hair trailed over her bare flesh. The cool silk of it dragged over her beaded nipples, down her belly, over the wet flesh of her pussy like a whispered caress.

A soft rush of breath left her lips and her eyelids slid down a bit, leaden. The man was a drug. Being with him changed her in elemental ways, healed hurts she'd thought were soul deep.

Sweet, carnal lips slid across her collarbone and then down to her nipple. Electric pleasure shot from her nipple to her clit. A moan dragged from her gut.

"That's more like it." His words were low, vibrating around her nipple.

Mei looked down the line of her body at his mouth on her nipple. It was shockingly erotic, his tongue curling around the tip. The sharp edge of his teeth against her skin made her gasp as shivers of delight broke over her.

She let go of the door to reach down and touch him but she found herself picked up and placed on the cool marble-topped table near the door.

"That's better," he murmured and dropped to his knees. Spreading her thighs wide, a grin split his face. "Such a gorgeous pussy. And all mine."

Leaning in, he took a long lick. Pleasure vibrated through her body and up her spine. "There are beds, you know," she gasped.

"I know. But I want to take you everywhere I can, in every way I can. Now hush, I'm busy."

She laughed for a moment. Until two questing fingers slid up into her and hooked to stroke over her sweet spot. Jumping in response, a startled cry came from her.

Card rolled his eyes to look up at her. As always, it seemed he looked right through her, right to her heart. He held her gaze as he loved her with his mouth, fucking into her with his fingers.

Her entire body began to shake with need as he quickened his pace on her. She finally broke away from his eyes, closing her own and leaning her head against the wall behind the table. Her hands sifted through the thickness of his hair, holding him to her as he feasted. Devoured. Worshipped her with his mouth.

A low, nearly feral groan came from her lips. He touched her so deeply, affected her. Saved her. Her body vibrated on a frequency just for him. When his teeth abraded her clit she arched as climax burst over and through her body.

Through a haze of intense pleasure she felt him stand up and take her lips in a kiss. Her arms automatically encircled his neck, holding on as he plundered. Her taste, mixed with his, was sweet on his tongue as he slid it against hers.

Big hands at her waist pulled her to the edge of the table and moments later he thrust his cock deep into her pussy. He swallowed her gasp of delight and caught her bottom lip between his teeth for long moments.

"You. Are. My. Everything." Each word was followed by a roll of his hips, sending the thick meat of his cock into her, slicing through the heated walls of her pussy.

"Yes," she moaned because there was no other answer.

He picked her up and moved her against the wall with force. An arm banded about her waist took the impact but she knew it was his way of underlining his words. "Yes. Damn it, yes. You were meant to be my woman. I touch you and I can smell your pussy bloom and get slick for me. For *my* touch. Your skin breaks out in shivers when I speak close to your ear. Your nipples harden when I look at you. And damn it, I only look at you. There is nothing else but you. But us. And now Jayce, but he's part of us too."

She moved her head from side to side, impaled by his cock as he pistoned into her body, held captive by his words. By the truth of them.

Lauren Dane

"And more than the way your body responds to me and mine to you, our hearts and souls are connected."

Mei looked deep into eyes that were more yellow than green, knowing he'd see right into her heart. A tear slipped free, clinging to her eyelashes.

A soft sound came from him and she felt his tongue capture her tear just at the side of her eye. The tenderness of the gesture tore through her and a sob broke free.

"Thank you. Thank you, Card for loving me. For making room in our lives for Jayce. You saved me and helped me love again."

"You don't need to thank me. I'm yours. I'm here. Where I've been from the first moment I saw you. I'm not going anywhere. Be with me." His soft words were murmured against her temple as he continued to stroke into her.

She wrapped her legs around his waist and put her head on his shoulder and let the tears come even as he healed her with each press into her body. Her arms clutched his biceps like a lifeline.

"Shhh. Oh my angel, you feel so good in my arms. Your sweet pussy was made for my cock, you fit me perfectly."

"I'm no one's angel." Her voice was tear-roughened. Shame pulsed through her at what had happened in Carthau.

"My angel. My heart. And you are. Give me your eyes, Mei. What happened to you does not make their perversity your fault. You know this. You are good. Strong. Beautiful."

Slowly, apprehensively, she opened her eyes and met his. Their gazes remained locked as he walked down the long hallway and kicked open the door to their room. Without leaving her body, he brought them both down to the mattress.

Looming over her, he took her in long, slow and deep strokes. He spoke in muted tones, half in English and half in the language of his origin. The words the pack spoke. It wasn't so much the words as the tone. He gentled her with his voice.

82

The fire of need build up in her body again. Oh how she needed to come with him embedded inside her. As if he'd read her mind, he changed his angle so the entire length of his cock brushed over her clit each time he pumped into her.

"Oh yes," she whispered as the spark of pleasure sent her into full conflagration. Mei writhed beneath him, arching to get more contact.

"That's the way, little warrior. Grab it, rub your clit on me. You're so wet, your honey is scalding hot. I can feel the walls of your cunt clutch me. So fucking good."

Mei was blinded in her need. He thrust into her and she rolled her hips, grinding her clit against him. Deep and hard her orgasm rolled through her, taking away power of speech and all thought as it sucked her under.

"Shit..." Card mumbled as she came around his cock. Moments later she felt the spasm of climax work through his cock as he came into her.

They remained locked for long minutes afterward, barely moving but occasionally rocked by another tremor of pleasure.

At long last he dropped next to her on the bed, throwing one arm over his head and grabbing her waist with the other, pulling her back to snuggle into him. She molded her body to his, relaxing into the hard warmth of his body.

* * * * *

Long minutes later Card plumped a pillow behind her and helped her to sit up. "Go on now. Magic up something tasty and be sure you get yourself some juice."

Drowsily, Mei rolled her eyes and smiled. "That was quite refreshing."

He laughed. "Good. I could take you three more times without breaking a sweat so you'd better get eating or Jayce will call me out for not making you eat and fucking you instead."

["\n"]}

That's how Jayce found them, sitting in bed, naked, eating burritos.

"Well now, I can see you took care of our girl while I was out." By the time he crawled into the bed with them he was naked too.

"What is this?" He pointed to the food on Mei's plate.

"Hollenbeck burrito from El Tepeyac. Card and I lived in East L.A. for a few years, nasty ghoul infestation out at MacArthur Park. Anyway, we sort of did our first years of duty out there. Had these burritos there every Thursday. Here, have a bite."

He looked dubious but took a bite and Card laughed at his reaction.

"Gods, this is good!"

"You've never had a burrito before? I'll have to take you there once this is over." Mei smiled, pleased that he enjoyed the food.

"I don't spend much time on Earth. When I'm there I'm usually in New Orleans visiting Con and Em. Lots of jambalaya and gumbo, no burritos. And goddess you look good naked."

Mei's eyebrows rose. "How did it go with my mother?"

"She couldn't do it either. Had the same problem you did with having the magic slip through her grasp. We managed to get her back safely without your assistance. I'm not quite sure what we did before you came along." He winked and she snorted.

"We should talk to Em and see if she found anything out and then meet with the truthseekers."

"Already scheduled. We meet in two hours. You done eating?" Jayce motioned to the mostly empty plates.

"Yeah. I was just...oh." Mei giggled as Jayce pushed her back to the bed, the plates disappearing as he did.

* * * * *

When the three of them appeared in Aine's audience chamber at the appointed time there was no denying the glow about Mei, and Aine didn't bother to hide her smile.

"Despite the seriousness of the situation, I do love having you back and so well loved by these men who so clearly belong to you," Aine murmured in Mei's ear as they embraced.

Em explained that there were many texts on the troll wars and she'd probably need a few more days before she could get through them all.

The truthseekers came in and told them that they'd found out at least two of the different universes the Dark Fae had been rifting to—Sh'har, populated by humanoids with magical powers and a taste for blood, and Aurelia, the world where the trolls had been banished to after the wars all those millennia ago.

"Well, that's troubling. The Sh'har are dangerous on the best of days. But the trolls? If they could rift to Earth, imagine the trouble, the damage they'd cause. We've got to stop them." Aine's forehead creased with concern.

"Well, we need a little reconnaissance then, don't we? I think I need to sift to Sh'har to see what's going on."

"I didn't just hear you say that." Jayce stood and faced her. "It's dangerous there, Mei. You'll do no such thing."

"M'kay, in the first place, I was a warrior here. Or did you forget we stood side by side on battlefields before? In the second place, I've been a warrior for the Balance for nearly two thousand years, I've done far more dangerous things than do a little sneaky peeky. I've even been to Sh'har before. In the third place, I survived a thousand years in a demon prison. I can handle this. And the last thing, you're not in charge of what I do. I am a warrior. I don't sit around and look pretty. I hunt things and then I kill them."

"Yes, I remember and I remember being beside you on that battlefield when you were so injured I thought you were dead. I recall it got you thrown into that damned prison!"

A sob broke from deep inside Mei and Card stepped to her. "Stop it now." He held a hand up.

"Why are you protecting her in this? She can't do this. You're supposed to love her. How can you risk losing her? I'll tell you what it's like to think your wife is dead, Card. Do you want to know firsthand? She's playing tough but she paid the price before. I don't want to pay that price again."

"Yes, I know I failed. I know my time there made me less of a person. I get that." Mei's voice was quiet and she tried to walk out of the room but Card wrapped his arms around her.

"Angel, he doesn't mean it that way." Card's protectiveness kicked into high gear. He knew how she felt about her time at Carthau, knew she felt responsible for what happened to her. Felt she'd failed and the torture and rapes were her fault because she'd been weak enough to get captured.

"What are you talking about?" Jayce moved toward her but Card turned and snarled, his beast rising to the surface, causing Jayce to stop in his tracks, shocked.

"I want to leave," Mei mumbled into Card's chest. "Please."

"Come on, angel. Let's get you back to our rooms so you can rest."

Aine stood, confusion on her face. "What is going on? Mei? Darling, what is wrong?"

Em trembled as she sat there, eyes glazed, filled with tears.

"I'm taking her out of here right now. Don't try to stop me. Just let it go for now." Card held Mei tight with one arm and warded Jayce off with the other. Con stood and watched, confused.

"What the hell is going on?" Jayce yelled and a look of rage crossed Card's face, so deep that the room silenced immediately.

"I said I am taking her out of here and to let it go for now." He pushed past Jayce while Con held Jayce's shoulder and they left the room.

"Home. Really home. Please, Card. I want to be in my own bed," Mei said softly. With a sigh, Card took her out into the garden behind their suites and she sifted them both back to their house in San Francisco.

* * * * *

Em stood up and put her hands in the air. In a strangled voice she called out for everyone to be quiet.

"She's in so much pain I'm shocked she can even function."

Jayce turned slowly. "What do you mean? Is she hurt? Why didn't she say so? Why didn't Card say so?"

"She's got no real physical wounds, Jayce. Her pain is in her heart and mind. She was fine really until you mentioned her being taken prisoner. She feels responsible. Dirty. She feels like she failed and got what she deserved."

"She feels responsible for what?"

"Her time there. In that hellhole. I felt flashes of what happened to her. It was… I don't know if I can even put it into words." She shuddered and Con put his arms around her waist, pulling her back to him.

"Mei thinks she deserved whatever those fucking animals did to her in that place? How could she? Why didn't Card tell her otherwise?"

Em shook her head. "Jayce, Card saved her. In more ways than one. The anguish he felt when she began to cry was nearly overwhelming. I'd bet anything he's been telling her from day one she wasn't responsible for what they did. But torture like that... Jayce, back in college I took a class, psychology of warfare. Torture humans are capable of can warp the person being tortured. But Carthau isn't a human prison, it's a prison run by demons. Imagine what a thousand years of constant pain and emotional manipulation can do to someone. But she survived because she's strong. We all have our weak spots, Jayce. Hers is this."

"So you're telling me what? To wave gaily as she heads off to another dimension on some dangerous mission? When I just got her back after thinking she was dead for three millennia?"

"You said you wondered how Card could just let her go?" Em sat again and the others followed suit.

"Yes. How can he love her and risk her that way?" Jayce's hands gripped his knees tight, knuckles white.

"He loves her enough to let her go and do her job. To show her his confidence in her. But he's her partner too, he's her backup. He walks a fine line but it's what she needs, Jayce."

"Em is right, Jayce." Aine wiped her eyes. "Knowing she blames herself makes me feel sick. My baby being harmed that way at the hands of my sister—I want to kill Eire myself! But Jayce, you need to get it together and work with Card to make Mei feel more secure. She's always been a fighter and if she's one of Carl's warriors she's more than capable of doing just about anything that gets tossed her way. I hate risking her too but in this we need to think about what's best for Mei."

"I don't know if I can just accept this. Her life in danger all the time? I love her. I just got her back."

"Jayce, you have no choice. Don't you see? If not, you're using this horrible feeling about herself against her. Work with Card, find a way to deal with this or you'll have a wedge between you and it'll rip you three apart." Con sighed. "She loves you. It's clear she has since you two started in the Favored together. You love her. I've been alive a long time and

I know a few things for sure. One of them, the most important one, is that love is worth the work." He looked to Em, who smiled over Elise's head as their daughter sat in her lap, playing with her bracelets.

Closing his eyes a moment, Jayce nodded. "I suppose you're right. It starts with finding her and getting back on track with her right now."

Aine waved toward the door. "Go on. Coordinate with Conchobar on the next steps. Keep me apprised."

Jayce nodded to Con and told him he'd be in touch after he spoke with Mei and Card and left.

But there wasn't anyone in their suite. Jayce looked around and didn't find a note either, grew more frantic.

Em and Con looked up, surprised when Jayce burst back into the room. "She's gone. They're gone."

"She couldn't have gone to Sh'har already. She would have worked with you, even if it was just to tell you to fuck off and go. She's been doing this too long to try to fly solo." Em looked to Con. "Let's check with the Donovan, maybe he knows something."

"I can't believe Card would help her run off. Damn it." Jayce slammed a fist into the arm of his chair.

"She said she wanted to go home. Maybe that's where he took her. Don't assume he helped her run off. He wanted to comfort her, make her feel better," Em said.

"I don't know how to get hold of the Donovan but Aine does. I don't know where their home is."

Em reached out, squeezing his hand. "Don't panic. Let's have Aine contact the Donovan and we'll go from there."

Several minutes later Aine came in, Carl Donovan at her side.

"I see you've run into Mei's weak spot. Go on and get her, she's most likely in San Francisco. She and Card have a home there." The Donovan gave Jayce their location and without another word Jayce sifted from the room.

Chapter Five

Card stood and went to the door when he heard the pounding. "Shut up and come in." He stepped out of the way to let Jayce through.

"Nice warding, I couldn't sift directly into the house. Where is she?"

"One of the Donovan's people did it. She's sleeping and you'll let her. I spelled her out because she damn well needs the rest. Sit down and we'll talk. Want a drink?" Card called back over his shoulder, walking into the kitchen and coming back with a beer.

"Why don't you just magic it?" Jayce nodded his thanks when Card handed him the bottle and sat.

"We try very hard to live a normal, as in human, life when we're not working. She likes it that way. I like it that way. Time spent gardening and cooking meals is good. The kind of tired you are at the end of a day at the flea market or laying a new path in the yard, that's healthy." Card narrowed his eyes as he sat back against the back of the chair. "But I don't expect you came all this way to talk about gardening."

"How is the time slip?"

"It's only been about four hours since we came back."

"How can you deal with it, Card? How can you let her go out and risk herself?"

"I'm going to tell you as much as I can. As much as I think she'll accept without truly getting upset or feeling betrayed over. So just sit back for a bit." Card took a long pull on the beer and toyed with the paper on the label as he began to speak.

"Her first five years or so after Carthau, she wouldn't let anyone touch her. Not a hug, not a handshake, nothing. She slept a lot, read. Worked on getting her magic back. She stayed with my parents at their home in Lycia. My mother is a healer in her own way and my pack took her in, made her their own.

"Anyway, Carl sent in an empath who helped Mei process a lot of what happened. She also saw a lot of healers who tried to deal with her internal injuries and the cold iron and burn wounds.

"I confess to you that I fell for her the first moment I saw her, nearly broken and chained to the floor of her cell. Her eyes, gods, her eyes held so much pain and hopelessness...but she fought her way out of there once I freed her. She had a spark then, just a tiny ember that has continued to stoke up to the flame you see today."

"What was it like after she returned from Tir na nOg thinking she'd been exiled?" Jayce asked.

"She was devastated and it set her back a ways in dealing with the emotional aftermath of her time at Carthau. It took me about ten years before she'd let me hold her hand. But I waited because, as you know, she's worth it. Another year before we kissed and it went like that until, well, anyway." Card blushed and Jayce snorted.

"It's odd to me that I'm not jealous that you helped her heal. I just wish I could have helped too. I'm glad she had you."

Card shrugged. "My mother told me, when I brought Mei to them after Tir na nOg, she said Mei was meant for me. I'd burned my way through females of as many species as I could before she came along. My mother was amused that I'd have to wait years to touch a woman. Mei taught me what it was to love. To put someone else's needs above my own. She taught me the meaning of forgiveness and strength and courage. And I adore her. I'd do anything for her, Jayce.

"It was clear pretty early on that the warden at Carthau had wanted to break her, to make her his pet." Card's voice hardened, roughening into a growl for a moment. "It was he who assaulted her most often. It was also obvious once she'd come out of there that she felt responsible for what happened. I understood it to a degree. A warrior taken prisoner feels like a failure to a certain extent. But from what the demon records say about the battle that day, she fought off a quarter guard of Dark Fae on her own, only being taken when she'd been injured so severely she couldn't move anymore from blood loss."

"She fought off fifty men?" Jayce asked in a whisper. "I was removed from the field by the medics and brought back to Tir na nOg. I..." Jayce's voice broke.

Card reached out and squeezed Jayce's knee. "I know. She does not blame you, nor do I. It was battle. Anyway, in all the years I've known and loved Mei, she has taken on the weight of what was perpetrated against her. Felt it was her punishment for being taken prisoner instead of dying on the battlefield."

Card looked Jayce in the eye. "You tell me, Jayce. If you knew the only way to help your woman fight her demons, in a very real sense, was to let her go out and physically right wrongs, wouldn't you? Would you try to make her into what she isn't in order to protect her physically while she died inside of guilt? Or would you serve as her partner and help her defeat the evil in the universes to help her process what happened to her? I know my answer and I think you need to figure out what yours is."

A tear dropped from Card's eye and, reaching out, Jayce thumbed it away. "I underestimated you," Jayce whispered.

Card shrugged as he pulled himself together. "I was the executioner for my pack for thousands of years. I tracked and killed. Should I tell you about the piles of skulls from my kills to let you know how tough I am? I know what I am, Jayce. I do not need to prove my masculinity to anyone and it does not make me less of a man to give my woman, *our* woman, what she needs. What kind of prick would I be if I had the need to prove myself at her expense? That's not a man.

"In answer to your question, I go with her. I'm her partner, her backup. I survive her need to avenge and kick the asses of the nastiest things in the known universes by being there. If she left and I had to wave as she did it and stay back, I couldn't survive it. I was already a warrior, so when she decided she wanted to join we became partners. It's the way I deal with it. I let go, but not all the way."

"I thought that would work. I was her partner and her backup but if you recall, I was with her that day in Sareem. I failed her."

Card threw his hands up. "I can only shore up one of you at a time. That was different. A battlefield is different than what she does now. You're not a superhero, you can't take responsibility for everything in the world. Not even Carl can do that."

Jayce laughed. "All right, all right. You have room on your team for one more?"

One of Card's eyebrows rose. "Are you serious? What about the Favored?"

"My cousin Cullen has been doing this for nearly as long as I have. Mei will spend time in Tir na nOg, I'm sure. When we're there, I'll stand at Aine's right hand. Con does well on a part-time basis. We can work it out and Aine will be all for it if it means Mei is safer in the field. I can't imagine she'll hang up her warrior shoes after we deal with the Dark Fae."

Card barked out a laugh. "No. No she won't. Our girl loves to kick ass." He stood. "I imagine you're tired. I know I am. Come on. Our bed is big enough for three. The bedroom is at the top of the stairs, first door on the right."

"Why'd you spell her down? She seems to get tired after using her magic. More quickly than I remember."

"You have no idea the physical damage they did to her, Jayce. You know the Fae gain vital energy from the earth and their surroundings. But she couldn't get that. Her cell was lined in cold iron, it sapped her of life for a thousand years. They fed on her terror and rage, her hopelessness and pain. She can snap the neck of a fully matured Macodemon guard. She can fight hand-to-hand with gargoyles and oathbreaker vampires and all manner of nasty things. But when she uses her magic it drains her. But you're not to say anything about it. She feels self-conscious about it enough as it is. You must know she'll push herself to the very limits of her energy before she'll rest. It's why I try to nag her to take breaks."

Jayce heaved a breath. "We're going to have to kill the things who did this to her."

"I've killed many of them. There are those out there still and I'd be glad of the assistance. But for now, I'm going to go speak with the guards before I come up to bed."

"Guards? Not very good, are they? I got to the door without a challenge."

Card snorted. "These are my men, hand-picked from my pack. They knew of your existence the moment you sifted onto the walk at the end of the block. They notified me immediately. If I'd wanted you dead, you would be."

"You're still close with your pack then? And apologies, they're fine guards."

"I'm part of the royal line, much like Mei is. Only my two older brothers are both full-blooded Were. They are next in line before me. Their mother died in a pack challenge before mine came to Lycia."

"I'd like to hear that story."

Card shrugged. "Ah well, it's a long one. But my father's birthday is approaching, I want to tell them of this new development face-to-face. Mei is one of the pack as well. Not just as my wife but when she lived there after Carthau my mother took her under her protection. You can meet them all then."

They looked at each other for long moments and Jayce was surprised to feel things stirring low in his gut. Stepping back, he nodded. "I'm going up. I'll see you in a while."

Card's smile was enigmatic. "All right then."

* * * * *

Jayce liked the feel of their house. Warm, filled with love. The art on the walls was vivid, modern. As he took the stairs up to the second floor, he felt her presence pulling at him. Felt his woman as she began to wake. He moved quickly to the door and let himself in quietly.

"Jayce?"

The tear-roughened voice tore at his heart. "I'm here, *a thaisce*.. Rest yourself. We'll talk more in the morning."

When he reached the bed she'd pulled the blankets back and he crawled in with her, seeking contact with her body.

Her fingertips traced his bellybutton. He tried to push his rising desire away but it was a losing battle. "Mei, I know you're tired. I'm sorry you felt the need to run. We can talk more in the morning."

"I didn't run. I needed to be home. I wouldn't run from you, Jayce. I love you. I'm sorry I disappointed you."

He rose above her then, looking into her eyes. "Mei, you didn't disappoint me. It isn't possible. I love you and I worry for you. But I understand, or I'm trying to understand, you need to do your job. And so we'll work out a way you can continue it. I can't promise I'll be happy about your risking yourself, Mei. I want to protect you. But I respect your abilities and I trust them. We'll work out the rest as we go along."

"You're okay with my being a warrior?"

Dipping his head, he captured her lips for a brief kiss. "You were when we were together before. You are now. Card says there's room for one more on your team so the three of us can be together. Here, in Tir na nOg, wherever. I just want us to be together and if we can do that in the field, I'm okay with that."

Jayce cocked his head as he heard heavy steps approaching. "Card is back."

"He's been at the bottom of the stairs for the last ten minutes."

"Am I so transparent?" Card asked as he came into the room.

"No, just good and kind and wonderful. Come on to bed, it's cold in here." Mei reached out and pulled the blankets back from the other side of the bed and after he'd tossed his clothes to the side he slid in on the side opposite Jayce.

"Are we all okay?" Card nuzzled Mei's neck.

"On our way there," Mei murmured before moaning softly.

"I think I know what might help," Jayce said with a grin.

* * * * *

The three sifted back to Tir na nOg early the next afternoon. Con grinned when he saw them enter the audience chamber.

"Things look considerably better than they did yesterday eve."

"Working on it." Mei grabbed a cup of coffee and sat across from her brother. "We'll be doing some recon in Sh'har. As the time doesn't slip there like it does on Earth, we know it's coming up on evening there. I want to go in when it's full dark, with some major camouflage spells working."

"If we go in a few hours after darkness falls, most of them will have fed and will be intoxicated. That'll buy us some time. As we don't have a lot of information except that the Dark Fae have been rifting there, we'll be starting from scratch so we shall see what we can see." Card watched Mei through his lashes.

"Before we do that, I'd like to go and see Finn and Magda if you think they're ready for me, Con. In the meantime, Jayce, you deal with your mother. You'll have to excuse my absence. Uh, I have to be elsewhere. Anywhere but there."

Jayce's mother had never liked her. She'd liked the royal connections, sure, but not that her son had married some rough-and-tumble warrior instead of a pretty, quiet Fae like she imagined herself to be. Mei held back her snort. The woman was Jayce's mother after all.

Jayce winced, not even trying to deny the woman hated her. "Okay, okay. I'll shimmer over to Finn and Magda's as soon as I'm done there."

"Mei, angel, I need to go home and tell my parents about all of this," Card said. "I don't want it to get back to them and have them hurt. It's been three days already."

"I want you to meet Finn too. As for telling your parents, I'll come as well. We've got some hours yet before we need to go to Sh'har. Let's go and see Finn and Magda and then we'll go to Lycia."

"I don't want to add to your list, sunshine, but Em's family will want to meet you as well. Jayce is like a member of their clan and they'll want to know you." Con winked. "You're a popular woman."

Mei rolled her eyes. "First things first. Finn and then Lycia. Then Sh'har. Let's come back here and see if you've got an update for us, Em. After this is all over we'll meet your Charvezes.."

Jayce pulled Mei to him, kissing her hard. "I'll be there in a bit. Don't leave for Lycia without me."

"Of course not! The pack will want to meet you as well, Jayce. You're bonded to us both, that makes you pack too. There may be a bit of an interrogation if they're not impressed with Card's explanation. But they'll warm up to you eventually." Mei hated that he might get a cool reception at first but it had to be done.

After shimmering, Mei was captivated immediately by Finn's meadow and the house on the shores of the lake. A big golden dog came galloping toward them as they approached. Con, Em and Elise waved and Finn came toward them with a grin.

His gaze flicked over Mei and then he stopped, staring. "Goddess! Mei? It can't be."

"It is and that's not the only surprise I'm bringing with me today, Finn," Con said.

Finn stared at Mei for long moments before hugging her tight. Magda came out of the house with the boys, who came to meet them. Magda appeared as thrilled as Finn and Con to hear the news and she agreed with Mei and Em that Con and Finn's mother should not be told.

As they sat on the dock of the lake, feet in the water, Jayce approached with a wave.

"Let me guess, she wants to throw me a welcome back party," Mei teased.

"Mei, she's happy you're alive. She might not like you but she doesn't hate you and didn't wish you dead. She's less than pleased to hear about Card but," Jayce shrugged, "she'll do her best to ignore it until children come into the picture and then she'll bring a whole new level of pain into my life."

Em whipped her head around to look at Mei but stayed silent. Mei hated the pity she saw there.

"Mei? A *thaisce*, what's wrong?" Jayce brushed the hair away from her face.

"We've tarried too long to go to Lycia. I'm sorry, Card. Let's go to Sh'har and then we'll go to see the pack." She stood.

"You're avoiding the question." Jayce glared at her.

"I don't want to talk about it just now. Please."

Card sighed and stood as well. "We'll deal with it later. I promise. For now, let's go."

"Why is it that he gets to know everything but I keep having to wait? It's not right, Mei."

Mei spun to face Jayce. "Fine. I can't have any children. The rapes were so brutal and they used cold iron on me, *in* me, my reproductive system was damaged irreparably. There. Now you know. Gee, do you feel special now that you have the secret I-married-a-woman-who-can't-have-children handshake?"

A collective gasp sounded over Card's growl.

"I'm sorry, I..."

"No! I know you love me and I know you just want to know what happened. But I don't need your pity, Jayce. I need for you to listen to me when I tell you I don't want to talk about something right now. I'm not hiding things from you but I'm not some kind of machine either, I can't just roll out a thousand years of agony for your entertainment whenever you feel the need. This isn't a contest between you and Card about who knows more than the other. *I'm* not some kind of game."

She turned on her heel and stalked off. Em raised her hand to stop the men and followed, Magda on her heels.

"Wait! Mei, please," Em called as she ran to catch up.

"Em, I really don't want to have a bonding moment right now. I'm sorry but I just can't." Mei stopped but she kept her back to her sisters-in-law.

"Mei, he just wants to know you. You have to share yourself with him," Em said quietly.

"I know that! I know he's upset and he has a right to be. I don't want him to feel like I'm hiding things from him. But there are things that take awhile to talk about. I can't just lay every damned horrible thing that happened to me out like a buffet."

"This is going to be tough for you and Jayce because he knew you before all this happened and Card knew you after.

There are going to be problems if Jayce feels like an outsider in your life. I can't say I understand because I don't. I couldn't possibly. But if you ever want to talk or need a shoulder please know I'm there for you."

"Thank you. I need to go now. It's time." She turned and looked past Magda and Em to Jayce and Card. "You two ready?" A brief moment later she wore dark, warm clothing and her hair was up and covered in a dark watch cap.

"Let's do this." Jayce strode to her, pulling her into his arms, kissing her hard and fast. "I love you and it's not entertainment to see how you've suffered."

Guilt speared through her. She reached up and traced the line of his jaw. "I'm sorry. I truly am. It was wrong of me to react the way I did. You didn't know and you wanted to. I lashed out and it hurt you and I was wrong. There are things," she shook her head, "things you need to know and I'll try to share them all with you as I can. But for now we need to focus. Let's do the camouflage spell."

He cocked his head and smiled. "Okay. I'll try if you will. Thank you for apologizing. I'm sorry if my questions hurt you."

She kissed him again, softly, and turned back to Card, holding her hand out to him.

Because Fae magic would be easily detected in a place where Fae rarely visited, Card did the spell with demon magic. They'd be visible to each other but no one else.

"Be safe, sister," Finn called out and Con raised his hand in goodbye as they sifted away from their meadow and into an alley in the capital city, Sh'mura.

* * * * *

The three of them crept out, carefully avoiding the knots of people walking in groups. It was quiet as their prime feeding time had passed by several hours and the edge of their blood lust would have been muted.

The city was built on multiple terraces, each one walled with guards at the entrance to the next level. Their culture was dominated by hierarchy and it was ruled on a very top-down basis. Each terrace held a different class of people—the higher you went, the higher the class.

At the base stood the commercial district, filled with storefronts, including a red-light district. During the daytime the city was dominated by the humans who served the Sh'hari. But after dark they faded away into their barracks-like dwellings just outside the main gates and the Sh'hari dominated, the higher castes taking blood from the blood workers in the lower castes.

Mei had tracked a Sh'hari mage down there five hundred years before and it didn't look like it'd changed much since then.

A glance up the road that led out of the center of town toward the palace and capital buildings showed lights on in both. It would be dangerous to shimmer the distance so they walked instead. The spell made them invisible but they'd still make noise if they tripped over something or coughed so they had to be very careful and keep stealth at the top of their minds. They knew most likely any involvement with the Dark Fae would be with high-ranking Sh'hari so the plan was to head upward to the palace.

Mei stopped when she spotted a group of Fae near the gates to the government level of the town. One eye narrowed, she moved closer, and the three of them followed the Fae through the large gates into the next level.

"I don't like it," one of the Dark Fae grumbled quietly to another of his group. "Bringing them into the mix will only make trouble. Lorcan can handle it. Why do we need them?"

"They're powerful. They hate the humans too. Why not let them join us?"

"Because they can't be controlled. They're not just going to let us run the show. Lorcan is playing with something not easily contained and if it gets away from him we're all doomed."

The other Fae shrugged uncomfortably. "Oh look, there's Rennie, let's see how the spell is working." The path leveled out and the Fae moved off, down toward an open space about fifty feet wide. Not much vegetation other than some straggly grass. The group moved toward three other Dark Fae clustered around what Mei could feel was a rift spot.

"That's one of Bron's cousins, Rennie MacAillen," Jayce murmured to Mei and Card. "The MacAillens have been leading the Dark Fae for centuries. I didn't even know of Lorcan until you dealt with him the other day."

Mei's face darkened as they moved in as close as they could to try to overhear what was happening. "There's a rift here. Not a stable one," she murmured to Jayce and Card.

Card's face hardened and Jayce nodded once before they turned back to listen to what the Dark Fae were saying.

The one they called Rennie shook his head and threw his hands up in frustration. "I thought you said you could do this!"

"It's a complicated thing, Rennie. It's not like making it rain or conjuring a mug of beer. But we were even closer this time than last. We kept it open for several minutes. Even moved Fae back and forth. It will happen. It'll stay open and stable. You have to be patient."

Rennie glared at the speaker and those other Dark Fae assembled there with him. "If we can't keep it open for longer than ten minutes we can't move in people from more than one universe. How many Fae did you move through in ten minutes? Can they run through in groups?"

The other Fae shook his head. "No. For now, the way the rift is opened, it's one at a time and there's a time lag."

"How many?"

"Two."

"You're telling me it takes five minutes per person to get through the rift?" Rennie's voice rose.

"Yes. It's complicated! You know that. The interruption in space-time with the spell as it is now takes up time."

"We don't have time. It has to be a completed spell, stable, so we can move thousands through at once. We have to open one to Aurelia where our Dark Fae brethren are, one to Sh'har and another at Carthau in the Third Level. Humans may be stupid but they will notice if we're all just standing around. It has to open, open and then open. No five minutes per person. This isn't some play spell, this is war."

"I understand that, Rennie. But you're tearing a hole in space-time. It's not something that any of us are taught, we're learning as we go. We'll get it. Each time we do it we keep it open longer."

"If we don't move by midsummer we'll have to wait another Earth year. Which means we have to stay there to watch the time. I am sick of Earth. I hate humans and I can't bear to be with them yet another year as we are exiled from what is rightfully ours! Tir na nOg should be ruled by a Faerie who understands that we are at the top of the food chain. Humans should be our slaves, not our friends. We've wasted enough time being benevolent to them. It's a waste of our time and magic. They drain us simply by existing. I want them taken care of! And don't forget that the matter leaking through the half-assed rift spells has now alerted Aine and her lackeys to our plans." Rennie began to pace.

"And you'd all do well to remember who is working with us now. He won't tolerate any mistakes and I can't save you if you're dead or in Carthau." With an anguished growl Rennie stomped away and despite her shock Mei followed him, Jayce and Card along with her.

They followed Rennie through the maze of paths and sentries until he entered the palace. Card gave the caution handsign and Mei slowed and focused. Hearing "Carthau" had shocked her for a moment but Card was right. It was time to listen and learn.

Mei's gut clenched when she heard Eire's voice complaining about something. They turned a corner and stood in the doorway of a dining room and Mei nearly fell to her knees when she saw Xethan sitting there at the table, sneering at her aunt.

Card's arm encircled her waist, holding her up as he took them a step back, out into the hallway where they could sift out immediately. Detection wouldn't matter once they were gone if they had to get out of there at a moment's notice.

"Majesty," Rennie said, bowing a moment before dropping into a chair at the table.

Eire fluttered her lashes at him a moment and Xethan's lip curled.

"Tell me, Rennie, how did the rift spell work?" Hamil, the leader of the Sh'hari, asked.

"We kept it open for ten minutes. Moved Fae back and forth between here and Earth. My people have assured me they'll have it stable in no time."

"In no time? What does that mean? You've had plenty of time to get this far. You're running out of time for the Earth year. If you don't get it working by midsummer you'll have to wait yet again before the stars and seasons are properly aligned to make the spell work. On top of that, your clumsy attempts have alerted the Messenger to the situation and he's reunited Mei NiaAine with her mother. You have no idea how much power she has. You fools have just put your biggest foe into play," Xethan growled, his eyes glowing yellow.

Mei shivered and Jayce put his arm around her other shoulder, looking confused.

"That's the warden of Carthau. He's the one who..." She broke off, unable to continue, and Jayce's face hardened. He got the idea.

"Respectfully, Xethan, you seem to have a mild obsession with the woman. You're not seeing the big picture. My niece is nothing. She's not even half my age. Her powers are still strengthening. Mine are far stronger." Eire waved his words away and took a drink.

Mei's eyes widened as she watched Xethan turn slowly toward Eire. She knew that face and didn't even take pleasure at the flash of movement and the resulting bloody lip her aunt sported.

"You are a fool. Why do you think I held her as long as I did without killing her, Eire? Why do you think the Messenger held her safely, training her? Why do you think they reunited her with her mother now? It's not just about her strength and power, although you underestimate it to your own detriment. It's about how her strength and power fits with her Fae and half-breed lovers'."

Mei strained to hear more even as her system screamed at her to get out and away from the man who'd tortured her for so long.

"I think you held her because you wanted her," Eire sneered as she dabbed the blood on her lip.

"Of course I did. Idiot woman, it's hard for me to believe you and she are related, you're such a mincing fool. She is beautiful, strong, desirable and would have bred me many fine children." He chuckled. "She'll be breeding no one's children now. But that does not negate her power in this scenario. The power of three, Eire, you bimbo. Threefold powers knotted together, threefold lives knotted together. It's older than time, the magic they'll wield." Xethan turned to Lorcan. "If you don't get these rifts working soon they'll figure it out and there'll be no defense against them."

"We need to go, the spell will begin to weaken soon," Card murmured in Mei's ear and she nodded. They backed out slowly and crept away, sifting once they got out of the palace.

* * * * *

They ended up back in Tir na nOg. Mei turned to Jayce. "We've got to tell my mother what is happening and get Em working on researching this whole old magic, threefold thing. And then we need to go to Lycia. I think we should petition the Were to be our allies in this."

Card nodded. "That's a good idea. Jayce, go and tell the queen. Mei, I'm going to go to Lycia now. You go and talk to Em, don't forget about the whole midsummer comment.. Come when you're finished." He looked back to Jayce. "And I can prepare them for you."

Jayce laughed. "Good goddess, things were so simple a week ago." He kissed Mei thoroughly. "But so much better now. Are you all right? It can't have been easy seeing him there."

With a shudder of revulsion, Mei nodded. "Yes. If the demons are involved this is even more complicated than I imagined. It's always so odd to me that he looks normal. Like a college professor. He's a sadist of the highest order and yet he's so buttoned-down and handsome on the outside."

"We fought off a demon Bron thought he'd enslaved a few years back, Con and I did. But it wasn't like this one back at the palace. It said it was a demon lord."

"Demons have a complicated hierarchy. Those who can be called and temporarily enslaved are demi-demons. They're not grounded and they have no ability to resist powerful spells that call them. Many demons are given demi status as punishment and they have to earn their way back to power and the ability to hold themselves to their planes of existence. A demon lord is one step away from gaining its full power back. Dangerous because it's so close to gaining independence again. Feral.

"It's complicated, but a being like Xethan got to his level of power and influence through the lives he's taken and the pain he's inflicted. He holds all the power of those in his tribe,

107

the largest and most influential tribe in demon culture. He can command troops of demons and even demi-demons if he chooses," Card explained. "Generally they like to keep to themselves. If too many outsiders understood how they worked it would endanger their species. It's one thing to know demons are bad and they like to torture and that kind of thing. It's another thing entirely for demons to align themselves on sides in a war with other magical species. Xethan walks dangerous ground here."

"Because he's obsessed with Mei. That much is clear." Jayce's face took on a dangerous look

Mei sighed. "Why? I don't understand. I refused every advance, I fought him every time he assaulted me. I never showed him any kindness or affection. He certainly never showed me any."

Jayce tipped her chin up. "This is not your fault so stop that thought right now. He's crazy and cruel but it's not hard to understand why he'd be captivated by you. Now go on, talk with Em while I brief your mother. I'll meet you both in Lycia."

Mei watched Card sift away and Jayce's retreating back as she headed toward the apartments Con and Em had taken while in Tir na nOg.

Em made her a cup of tea as she explained everything they'd heard.

"Believe it or not I do know something about this. My sister and her husbands— she's got two as well—used the magic of three some years back to defeat a demon and fallen god. Why don't you three come back here when you've spoken with Card's pack? I'll head home and get the texts out and talk with Lee about it. I'll also look into the time issue. It's not unusual for magic to be strongest at certain times of the day or year. Each solstice is powerful, Samhain when the veil is thin, that sort of thing."

"Maybe if we can hold them off until midsummer we'll have a bit of room to wipe them from all the known universes."

Em grinned. "I do so appreciate how bloodthirsty you are. These bastards need to be taken out. They took my baby and they're trying to harm my entire species. Kick their asses, Mei."

Laughing, Mei leaned in and hugged Em before going outside to a safe sifting point and heading to Lycia.

Chapter Six

ᔥ

Card sifted into the alcove of his parents' home and was greeted by a dozen or so siblings all shouting his name and delivering caresses, kisses and hugs.

"Cardinian, my beautiful boy, come and say hello to your mother."

Card looked around the throng of his siblings and into the face of his mother. A full-blooded, high-ranking demon, she stood just four and a half feet tall. Waist-long hair, white as snow, was captured in a braid. Yellow eyes smiled back at him through a face as pale as her hair.

He moved to her and fell to his knees, face-to-face. "*Aloo, Mameri..*"

She kissed his temples and hugged him. "*Aloo*, Cardinian. And where is my daughter?"

"She's in Tir na nOg and will be here shortly. I have a lot to tell you and Dad."

"Sounds like it. Come on then, he's just had dinner and a few ales so he's in a good mood. I just finagled a vacation out of him." She winked and he laughed, following her into their living room where his father, the Alpha of the Leviathan pack, sprawled on a chaise, a chessboard on a low table between him and Card's oldest brother Pere.

"Card, come give your old father a kiss then," Cross called out as Card entered the room.

He did as he was bid and followed with a hug for his brother before sitting at his father's feet.

"Where's my lovely daughter?"

"She'll be here soon. Dad, I've got a lot to tell you so let me just start at the beginning. Let me finish before you start to ask questions, all right?"

Pere looked at his brother seriously and sat back to listen. Cross waved a hand for his son to continue.

True to his word, with the exception of a few growled outbursts, Cross held his tongue until the story was over and Card shrugged to indicate he was finished.

"That's a lot of action for less than a week." His father interrogated him for the next twenty minutes with unrelenting questions, some very intimate ones. Card answered them all as honestly as he could, knowing his father asked not only as a parent but as an Alpha.

"Truth is, son, it'll probably take three men to handle our Mei. If you're accepting of this, how can I not be?"

Card laughed and his heart eased when feminine laughter joined his as Mei entered the room and was immediately beset by his family with demands for hugs and kisses. He was relieved to see none of them held back or seemed upset by her having another mate. Then again, Were culture often embraced family units of multiple mates and so it probably wasn't so hard to understand. And they loved Mei, had done since the moment he brought her, broken and sad, to their doorstep those two millennia before. She was one of them and they seemed to understand she would never do anything to intentionally hurt him.

He watched as his mother put her hands to either side of Mei's head and eased her pain of seeing Xethan. She murmured into Mei's ear and Mei nodded and kissed his mother's cheeks before seeking out his father.

"Hello there, pointy ears. I'd ask how you are but I've heard the story. Busy girl." Cross winked. "Of course we'll get your back in the coming confrontation. Pere will get our troops battle ready.. Card tells me you saw the butcher, I'm sorry, pet. If I catch him first I'll kill him twice for you."

Mei folded herself to sit next to Card and put her head on Cross' thigh, sighing. "I've missed you all. Do you hate me for finding Jayce and going back to Tir na nOg?"

A collective gasp sounded and aural chaos ensued as a dozen people began to chastise Mei for even thinking it. Laughing, Card kissed the top of her head. "For a woman who is so very smart, you can be so dumb."

"Amen. Now, pointy ears, I've interrogated my son and he tells me he's accepted your bond with Jayce. He tells us that Jayce is bound to you both and that this Fae loves you and is worthy. If the story had been different, I may have had a little set-to with this Fae but if Card can live with it we can too. And I ought to wash your mouth out for even suggesting we'd be anything but overjoyed at your reunion with your mother. It doesn't signify what you are to us. You're still my daughter, that won't change. Not ever." Cross smoothed a hand over her hair.

Card smiled when he heard Jayce's arrival. "He's here. Now everyone behave and be welcoming."

Mei stayed seated at Cross' feet and let Card get up to greet Jayce. She wanted to let Jayce enter on Card's welcome, setting both men as equals and also respecting Card's station.

Jayce entered and dropped a fresh kill at Tila's feet. Mei watched, impressed that he knew the old ways and honored the wife of the Alpha with meat for her clan. Tila smiled, her sharp teeth looked slightly scary but her eyes were friendly enough.

"I bring meat for you and yours and ask for a place at your table." Jayce went down to one knee and Mei heard Cross' grumble of approval at her back.

"You are welcome at our table and in our halls." Card held his hand out, helping Jayce to stand. "Well done, Jayce."

Card turned and presented Jayce to the family. "This is Jayce MacTavish, my bond mate and husband and bond mate to Mei."

Mei stood and went to them, hugging them both tight.

Cross narrowed his eyes at Jayce for long, silent moments. "You have plans to take Mei away from us? To have her all to yourself in the Isle of Fae?"

"No sir. I love Mei and I understand her feet are rooted firmly here, as they are in Tir na nOg. I respect that and her place with you and I hope to find a place here as well."

"And how do you feel about Card?"

Jayce looked to him. "He is my mate. I honor his place at Mei's other side."

"Would you give your life for him?"

"I would give my life for him as I would for Mei."

With one short nod the tension in the room eased. "Welcome to Clan Leviathan, son. You are always bid welcome at our table and in our halls."

"Come on then, have you eaten? Mei, you look thin. Have you been taking care of yourself and drinking the tea I sent to you?" Tila took Mei's hand and pulled her down the hall toward the large kitchen where more children, grandchildren and extended family had gathered.

A brief explanation was made while Tila ladled stew into bowls and bade them to sit down while she bustled and got them bread, butter and ale.

"Oh this is so good, *Mameri*," Mei said as she tore off a piece of bread to butter. "I never eat this well anywhere else. Even magic can't make stew as good as yours."

"Flatterer. You already have my son, what else can I give you?" Tila winked and looked to Jayce. "You may call me *mameri* too when you feel comfortable with it."

"That's an endearment that means mother?"

She nodded and Jayce grinned. "Thank you, *Mameri*."

"Will you stay the night then, pet?" Tila topped off their mugs of ale.

"We need to be off to Tir na nOg first thing but yes, if Card and Jayce don't mind I'd like to sleep here."

Tila turned and gave quick orders to have their apartment readied. "You must come back to stay a few weeks when this is over. I've got a new loom and you're the only one with a quick enough hand to help."

"All the rugs you see on the walls and floors here are ones *Mameri* has made. She's very creative. I've yet to see her not be good at something she puts her hand to."

Jayce looked around the large, warm space and sighed happily. He did not grow up in a house warm with love and family. His mother would lose her mind at the very idea of eating at a table in the kitchen with a dozen other people milling around much less hand looming a rug or letting anyone call her an endearment. Aine had been more of a mother to him than his own had and in that moment, as he watched Tila take care of Mei, he was thankful Mei had had this after the hell of Carthau.

Pere came in a few minutes later and told them he'd called for troop readiness and that there'd be a meeting first thing in the morning of all the military leaders. They would stay for that to brief them before going to Tir na nOg to see Em.

"Before going to bed I'd like to take a walk by the lake. The fresh air will do me some good I think. You want to come with me?" Card asked them both and they agreed.

Mei had changed into a soft pair of pants and a red sweater and Jayce changed into jeans and a sweatshirt much like what Card was wearing. The three of them, hand in hand, took a winding path, the scent of clean water and fresh air taking all the kinks out of Jayce's muscles.

He was so used to using magic to do everything he'd missed out on simple pleasures like taking a walk and listening to the sound of a big pot of soup bubbling on a stove.

"This is a good life. Do you spend a lot of time here?" Jayce asked Mei as they walked.

"About four months a year or so. We have a small apartment here in the main house, on the main floor. Another four months in San Francisco and the rest of the time working or traveling. We'll of course spend time in Tir na nOg now. Do you still have our house?"

Jayce shook his head. "No. I couldn't bear it after a while. Your presence was everywhere and it hurt too much. I'm sorry. I've been living in the barracks but I have a house. We should get a place of our own though."

"Ah, your bachelor digs won't accommodate us all?" Mei winked and he felt a blush heat his cheeks.

"I didn't know, I swear to you."

Mei stopped and cupped his face between her hands. "I know you didn't. I don't begrudge you the love you may have felt when you thought I was dead. I'm just teasing you. If you like your house now we can expand it. It's not like we can't magic it larger."

He shook his head. "No. I want a place that's all ours. And I don't want to live in Tir na nOg full-time either. I find I enjoy the more simple life you and Card lead. I quite like the idea of laying a garden path and watching you make bread."

"She makes a very fine loaf of bread for someone who didn't know how to cook when I first met her." Card kissed her hand.

"We've got time."

"There are children who need to be loved, you know," Jayce murmured. "I've always seen you with children around. We can adopt a child. The thing that matters most is love, not how we get there."

Mei sighed and they started walking again. "We didn't know until about a thousand years ago that I couldn't have children. The damage, well, The Bona Dea couldn't even help. Card and I had such a busy life, and a dangerous one, that we sort of put it off for a long time. It wasn't until very recently that he and I had started to talk about the possibility of adopting a child. We can talk about it more after we've dealt with this rift business. If that's all right with you two?"

Card nodded and Jayce followed suit, satisfied for the time being.

"I find myself needing you two very much right now," Mei said, looking out over the water.

Jayce looked over her head at Card, who raised one corner of his mouth in a grin. "Then let's get back to our bedroom, shall we?"

As he walked quickly, desire heated Jayce's bones with the passage of time and distance until his hands nearly shook with need once they were back in the house and the door to their apartment closed and locked.

With a quick thought, dozens of lit candles filled the room.

"You're very crafty when you're horny, Jayce." Mei cocked her head and looked his way.

Surprise crossed his face and then he laughed. "In your presence I'm always horny. A man has to think on his feet with you around."

"Is that so? Hmm. That's where you want to be then? On your feet?" Mei thought her clothes away and stood there, naked, eyebrow arched.

Card chuckled darkly, watching them both.

"Oh you're in trouble now, Mei." Jayce growled low and circled her, still clothed.

"I do hope so. If I recall correctly, someone promised me a spanking not too long ago."

He stopped and looked into her face. "You're awfully saucy. I like it."

"I'm a naturally saucy woman. Anyway, you talk too much." She fell to her knees before him.

"Well," Jayce murmured, pleased.

"Indeed." Her hands made quick work of the button and zipper of his jeans and yanked them down.

"You could spell away the clothes."

She looked up at him and smiled slowly. "I could but that wouldn't be as fun. Jayce, it's like long walks and making bread, some things are better done the human way. Sometimes drawing out the touch, the time, the sensation of the whole experience is well worth it."

Taking his cock into her hands, she licked up the length of him, swirling her tongue around the head. The salty spice of his taste trickled through her senses, conquering her little by little.

She took him into her mouth then, slowly. Her knees rested against his pants as they pooled around his ankles. The feel of his zipper pressing into the skin of her calf made her feel alive, that edge of pain made the moment more real.

Her palms brushed up the wiry hair of his legs, over the hard muscles of his thighs. Those same muscles jumped at her touch, responded to her. She moaned her pleasure around the cock in her mouth and he hissed.

"Great goddess, Mei, you feel so good. You're so beautiful there, long and lean and supple. That you'd get on your knees for me... You devastate me. There's nothing before you." His hands were reverent on her head, fingers sifting through her hair.

"Mei, my angel, you have no idea what it does to me to see you there, kneeling, our mate's cock in your mouth. I've never been this turned on in my life," Card growled and moved to Jayce's side, into her line of sight.

A shiver broke over her and she whimpered around Jayce's cock.

"You like what you see, Card?" Jayce murmured.

"Gods yes," he answered.

Mei's eyes widened as Jayce reached out, wove Card's hair through his fingers and pulled him close enough to kiss. And what a kiss. Moisture pooled in her pussy as she looked up the line of Jayce's naked body, watching the sensual dance of lips and tongue and teeth as each of her men learned the other.

Jayce released Card, who stood back, chest heaving.

"Get to work, Mei. I'm going to fuck you very soon," Card said in a low, desire-rough voice.

A shiver of his own worked through Jayce as he licked his lips, Card's taste still there, feral and wild. He'd never kissed another man before, never wanted to, but as he'd stood and listened to Card speaking to their woman he'd wanted it with powerful force. And it had been good, shockingly good. He wasn't sure he'd ever desire Card on the same level he did Mei but something had awakened with the spell Freya performed and he wasn't afraid to see where it led.

Jayce looked back to Mei, watching her rock back and forth as she took him into her mouth over and over. Her movement was rhythmic and each time her lips enveloped him, tongue soft and wet sliding over his cock, he felt it draw his body ever closer to climax.

This beautiful woman there at his feet, her hair soft over his hands and arms, her mouth on his cock — it was so much to him. *She* was so much to him. Never in his very long life had he felt so tender toward anyone else. She owned his heart.

He drew closer and closer to climax and he tried to pull back but she held on to his thigh, hand still wrapped around the base of his cock.

"Mei, I'm going to come."

She rolled her eyes up and looked into his, the ties between them stretched and pulled taut and brought them closer. He wasn't even sure what the hell it was but it felt earth-shattering. He felt like he'd just walked inside her and she'd let him.

His head fell back as the pleasure rocked him. He locked his knees and tightened his thigh muscles. Hands in her hair holding her close, he came into her, his life and commitment and love pouring out of him and into her.

She stood and he felt his clothes spelled away and he opened his eyes, watching as Card led her to the bed. "Now's the time to spell the clothes away," she said in a murmur.

He fell back onto the ridiculously luxurious bedding on the gigantic bed. Quickly, as he fell he reached out and brought her down with him, in turn bringing Card as well.

"As soon as I can move again, you're in for it."

"Talk, talk, talk," she said with a laugh. "Oh, and just a note, that kiss? Wow. Just wow. Please feel free to do it again and again after that. I don't think I ever really got how hot two men could be together. I *so* do now."

Card rolled her over, lightning quick, pinning her beneath his body. "We'll keep that in mind. For now, spread those long legs for me, Mei."

Her heart stuttered and she obeyed. His mouth found hers for a brief time, pressing a kiss to it. "Mmm, you taste like Jayce." Mei heard Jayce gasp even as she did. Card's lips moved down her neck, over her collarbone and down the valley between her breasts.

The heated wet of his mouth found her nipples until she writhed beneath him, soft moaning sounds coming from her lips. And he left a cool, wet trail as he kissed and licked down her belly, coming to a stop as he got comfortable between her thighs.

Card had a nice, meaty cock and could fuck a woman until she couldn't think straight but what she really loved was that he was a genius at oral sex. The man didn't just excel at eating pussy, he was a fucking pussy-eating virtuoso. Yes, she'd done it with Jayce, who certainly had skill and enthusiasm, but Card felt like a day wasn't complete without going down on her and there was something really wonderful about a man who clearly thought she was the best-tasting thing that ever lived.

Settling in, he winked at her just before taking a quick lick, making her jump and then moan. Strong, big hands held her thighs not only open but spread flat against the mattress so that she had to arch into his mouth. She was wide to his touch, bare and vulnerable, and she had to close her eyes against it.

Jayce moved down her body to lie beside Card and watch. A surprised cry came from her but Card's hands held her wide, not letting her close herself to them.

"I've never tasted a pussy as good as this one. I could bury myself in her five times a day and it wouldn't be enough," Card told Jayce.

"Yes, sweet, a bit salty. Don't be selfish now, let me have a taste." Jayce pushed in and suddenly two tongues slid through her and she had to bite her lip to keep from screaming.

Which did nothing to stop the torrent of pleasure they unleashed in her. Each lick was in vivid color against the back of her eyelids. Each flick against her clit shot sparks up her spine. When Card pushed one finger and then another inside her she whipped her head from side to side, glad her hair covered part of her face from him. She knew she must wear a look of sheer need, of desperate yearning to be devoured by them. Possessed. Wanting nothing more than to be with them, to be there for their touch and to touch them both. It was all-encompassing and she didn't have enough words to express how much it was to her.

Relentlessly, each man loved her with his mouth and hands, one still holding her at her hip, the other with fingers slowly fucking into her as they licked and kissed her pussy like a lover.

When she came it sucked her down and under. She couldn't hear, she couldn't speak, she only felt as the shock of overwhelming pleasure shot through her body. Her back bowed and a hoarse shout came from her lips.

Several long moments passed as her muscles jumped and her pussy fluttered. "Now, I've been thinking that you need two cocks buried deep in you at once." Card ran calloused fingers down her belly and suddenly she found herself face down on the mattress, Jayce's hair brushing down the line of her back like a caress.

"Card, lie down so Mei can wrap her pretty little cunt around your cock."

Card scrambled to lie down and Mei watched him, a smile on her lips.

"Ride him, *a thaisce*. And then I'm going to take you from behind, Mei."

His words were the barest whisper next to her ear as he moved her, pulling her up by her hips. She scrambled atop Card as he held his cock at the right angle. They both sighed with satisfaction as she pushed back into his touch, taking the blunt head of his cock into her pussy.

A ragged gasp tore from her as he thrust inside, hard and deep in one movement. He stilled again and there was nothing but them. Nothing but their breathing and the beat of their hearts. His fingertips softly traced over the curve of her hips and then down over her ass and the backs of her thighs.

"Now," Jayce settled in at her back. "It's my turn." He traced fingertips down her spine and she arched back into his touch. Reaching around where she and Card were joined, he pulled her lube back and traced slowly around her rear passage.

"I don't know about this, Jayce. I've never done this."

He laughed. "I've been in here myself, Mei!"

Card and Mei both laughed in response. "No, not *that*. I've done that before. I mean the whole double penetration stuff."

"Well, that's good. But I want to be inside you when Card is inside you. I need it. Let's take it slow. If it doesn't work, we'll stop."

Card dragged out and pushed in again. At first slowly. As if by a whim instead of in any rhythm. "You feel so good, Mei. I want this feeling forever. Just you and me and Jayce here, your pussy hugging my cock, the scent of your desire on my hands and lips. Your taste burning into my very soul."

A ragged sound came from her gut when Jayce's slick fingers breached her slowly and carefully, stretching her. She heard the sound of a lid snapping open and then things were even slicker as he worked lube into her before the head of him was there, pushing into her body.

"Gods!" Card cried out as her cunt tightened around his cock.

It felt as if she were drowning in them, surrounded by so much masculinity she couldn't quite take a breath. Her body was full, overfull, and it was all she could do to simply hang on as the two of them found a rhythm, seesawing into her around each other's thrusts.

Mei reached back and touched Card where their bodies met, down around his cock until she held his balls in her palm. A smile curved her lips when she heard his muffled hiss of pleasure. Her other hand reached up and wrapped around Jayce's neck.

She didn't have words for them. Not in the same way Card had for her. Card who never failed to praise her as a woman and a warrior. Not the same as Jayce, who'd been working so hard to try to accept his new position in her life. But she could show them with her body how she felt. Show them how much they pleased her, made her feel sexy and beautiful and strong. She didn't have to fear these men thinking she was too strong or too tall or too rough. They appreciated it, had their own strong, tall and rough and met hers with it without reservation.

Card looked up into her face. Watched the flush move up her body. Her eyes were closed, her golden hair cloaking her skin as he made love to her for long minutes, slowly bringing her up as he brought himself up. Behind her Jayce, his face set in concentration, his braids swinging back and forth as he moved. Card wished he could see what the three of them looked like from afar, this beautiful creature writhing in pleasure between these men who adored her so.

His hands smoothed down the line of her back, brushing against Jayce, over the flanks of her legs and up to her breasts, taking them into his palms.

Moving a hand up, he traced the seam of her mouth until she sucked his fingers inside. He gasped and then took them away, bringing them to her clit. Pressing over her gently, he made her come again before beginning to speed his thrusts.

"Oh hell, that's it, I can feel her pussy clamping down on you," Jayce gasped.

It was all she could do to hold on to them as they increased the speed of their thrusts. Orgasm still claimed her as the overwhelming sensations of two men invading her body rolled through her, stealing speech and thought. Over and over the sounds of their union rang through the room over soft sighs and moans until first Jayce pushed deep and came with a tortured, deep moan of her name and Card followed.

She slumped to the side as each man got up and then came back to her shortly. Jayce picked her up and followed Card into the bathroom where a steamy bath waited.

"Sometimes you can have a mixture of Faerie magic and the human way, yes?"

She smiled up at him and then over to Card as she stepped into the hot water and sank down with a satisfied sigh. "Absolutely. You two coming in?"

"Definitely. I like you wet. In all guises." Jayce's leer made her warm all over again.

Snorting, she moved until they got into the giant tub.. One on either side of her so she could touch them both, her head on Jayce's shoulder and her legs on Card's lap.

They soaked until the heat leeched from the water. Once they were tucked into bed, the warmth of the comforters creating a cocoon around them, Mei drifted away and into sleep. Jayce looked to Card, who was still awake, and motioned toward the doors that led to the terrace outside the room.

The two of them quietly got out of bed, dressed and headed out where they could speak without waking Mei.

"So tell me what you know of this Xethan." Jayce sat on a bench and looked out over the vast wooded grounds, silvery in the moonlight.

"It's always been my feeling and my belief, after reading the logs I stole the day I freed Mei from Carthau, that he is more than obsessed with her, he's in love with her. Demon males may lust lightly but they don't love that way. Once they love, they love bone deep. But a full-blooded demon male facing unrequited love would eventually move on and focus that attention on another. If he could." Card shrugged. "Mei is, well, you know what she is."

"This war isn't about domination of the Fae or of humans for him. It's about Mei."

Card exhaled sharply. "Yes. After hearing him tonight, that's what I think as well."

"Do you think she can handle this?"

"I don't know. She's so strong. Her will to survive is so strong. I'd like to think so. But tonight when she saw him she nearly lost it."

"But she didn't." Jayce couldn't keep the pride from his voice.

"No and that gives me hope. We need to kill him. Even if the Dark Fae get away with this, we need to kill Xethan." Card's last words were little more than a growl.

"Yes." A ferocious light shone in Jayce's eyes, matched by Card's expression. "But these Dark Fae are responsible for her time in Carthau and they have to go too. Every. Last. One."

"Card my man, I like the way you think." Jayce laughed and they stayed out there, planning and talking for another hour or so before joining their woman in bed and falling asleep, the scent of lovemaking still in the air.

* * * * *

Xethan walked the battlements around the palace as the sun rose, thinking about Mei. He'd been foolish tying his future to these Dark Fae. They were running into the wall between the worlds that would fall on the day after midsummer, August 22 in Earth parlance. While sifting would still be possible, a rift would not as the universes aligned in a way that made the spell impossible to work.

And worse, he knew the instability of the partially opened rifts would worsen and it was quite a possibility that there wouldn't even be an Earth by the time late spring rolled around, enabling the rift magic again.

But he couldn't resist the chance to have her again. Mei was the most magnificent woman he'd ever met. That she'd withheld a thousand years worth of torture and manipulation without breaking was a testament to her ability and inner strength. His body ached for her as he thought of her face, the stubborn set of her jaw. She'd hated him and that hadn't been his plan at all. He'd wanted her devotion but she wouldn't yield and so he took what he could by force. Stupid, that, it just made her hate him all the more, but he couldn't resist her.

This time he'd have her or she'd die. The thought of her being in any other man's bed had rode him hard over the last two millennia since she'd been freed. Worse, knowing a half-breed was the one she shared her heart with made him livid. The half-breed didn't deserve a female like Mei. And now the Fae as well, the one who'd been her husband before.

125

Xethan went back into the palace through a casement window on his way back toward his rooms. He'd rest and head back to Carthau to check in.

Outside the dining hall he stopped, head cocked, taking a deep breath. It couldn't be. It was just his imagination, after all he'd been thinking of her so much she was imprinted on his senses.

On a heaved sigh, he continued on his way to his bed.

Chapter Seven

ॐ

It never failed to impress Mei when the ranks of all the packs in Lycia gathered for a council meeting. The council space was easily ten thousand square feet and open at least three stories to exposed rafters.

Cross Leviathan stood at the head of the room, half a foot taller than every wolf gathered there. He rivaled Aine agewise, having lived and led his pack and these wolves for nearly thirty millennia.

Five thousand pack leaders and their seconds stood in row after row, all facing their Alpha. Male and female, all the largest and strongest of their clan, all battle hard with the light of ferocious loyalty in their eyes.

The scent of pack permeated the space, of forest and loam and that spice of musk and fur. It stirred Mei's blood.

Cross' deep voice vibrated off the timbers of the open space as he told them all about the growing threat of a united demon and Dark Fae force.. He asked for their pledge to ally with the Fae, to protect the humans and other creatures across the known universes, and they responded, raising their voices in a howl that shook the rafters.

Pere walked among them, next in line to his father's seat, and Mei saw how much they respected him.

The leaders of each pack pledged their protection to Cross before sitting and waiting for orders. Pere addressed them, telling them to make ready for war. Setting up schedules to train. Mei knew it was a formality, the Were kept in shape, kept ready, they had as long as she'd known them. Still, knowing she had their numbers to add to the Fae made her heart glad.

Jayce, as the Chief Councilor and the head of the Queen's Favored, stood and thanked the gathered Were for their allegiance and strength. They all watched, as did Mei, as he paced the dais. He'd changed into a kilt branded with the queen's colors, her familial colors. Strong, muscular legs showed as he moved and Mei felt a bit faint at such a display of masculinity.

His deep red hair moved like a living thing, warrior braids swinging. With a single growling howl they accepted him and that great sword at his side and Mei let go of the breath she'd been holding. The parts of her life were all coming together and she was so grateful for it.

* * * * *

After the meeting they said their goodbyes and headed back to Tir na nOg.

Con greeted them at the front door to their suite of rooms at the palace, grinning as they entered. "Hello, come on in. Em is just getting Elise down but she should be out in a moment."

They sat in the living room and talked strategy for some minutes before Em joined them, sitting next to Con with a grin. "My family is dying to meet the mystery woman! I saw them all earlier when I sifted home to do some research and they're all abuzz with the news."

"Mystery woman?"

"I had to promise everyone that you'd come visit after all this craziness and let us throw a big party. I think the entire Charvez clan with all our husbands and my mother, aunts and grandmother would be overwhelming just now." Em laughed. "My sister Lee said, 'We didn't even know Jayce had such a dramatic past. And Con with a sister even.' They're anxious to welcome you to the family."

"Glad to know you spoke of me often," Mei said dryly, a bit hurt.

"Don't go making a big deal of this, Mei," Card murmured in her ear. "He thought you were dead, it probably tore him up to speak about you."

"Okay, well, Em, you said you had something to tell us?" Mei said, clearing her throat.

"Yes. There's old magic. Magic that is without words or form. Fae magic has a lot of this type of magic embedded within it. Your magic is inherent, you simply think it and it comes to be. Well, depending on each person's set of gifts and power level, yadda yadda. Anyway, the power of three is incredibly strong. With my sister and her mates it was the melding of blood and her earth magic and Alex's arcane magic. The marrying of that made them into a single unit and Lee was able to harness all their strength and make it her own when she fought Angra and the demon lord who tried to break the Compact that gives us our power.

"And this is what I think you three need to do. Jayce and Mei have Fae magic but more than that, Mei is a Warrior for the Balance. Her magic is changed because of that. She's been trained and honed by the one you call the Donovan and the one we call The Messenger. Card is half demon, half Were. His powers are two-fold and he's also a warrior. You all share your quest for justice with a sword and you all possess magic and are tied by a bond created by the one who created our Compact. Freya's magic is unique, older than time, and I suspect this spell she created for you has enabled you all to share in and truly become a magical triad. Grounded power, mystical power and the power of animal. Join those threads together and the three of you are formidable enough to stop an army set on destroying humanity and unseating a Fae queen."

Mei sat back and took it all in, nodding. "It makes sense I suppose. A witches knot, right?"

Em nodded. "Exactly. That's exactly it. I think Freya's spell created the medium and I've taken the liberty of writing a spell of my own that should bring it all together nicely."

Mei laughed. "Em, is there anything you aren't good at?"

"If there is, I haven't seen it yet," Con said proudly.

"Not that he's biased or anything," Jayce said with affection.

"Have you three, uh, well, good lord, I don't know how to ask this politely so, have you three climaxed at the same time, as in all had sex at once?" Em's face burned bright red.

Mei chewed on her bottom lip for a moment, caught between laughter and embarrassment. "Yes. Man, I can't believe I'm talking about this in front of my brother.."

"Okay, I'd sort of made that assumption when I wrote the spell so the sex part isn't necessary. Instead I grounded it with blood. Earth magic."

"Where do we do this?" Card asked.

"Here, I think. The palace and grounds are all very well warded. Aine's private gardens just outside her private rooms have a magical circle. I've practiced there so I know it's effective. You need bare earth and naked sky for this one," Em explained.

"Well, let's do it." Mei stood, Jayce and Card following.

"You should be skyclad for this. We'll all set the corners in the yard but you'll be alone in the circle and that part of the yard. I'm going to let Cian know we're leaving, he's here to hang out and guard Elise in case she wakes up and then we can go."

On the way to the private gardens, Em explained the elements of the spell. Once they went outside she and Con took opposite sides of the circle and set a protective spell of their own.

Once she saw Con and Em turn their backs and set the protective spell, Mei magicked off their clothes. The evening breeze was a warm caress against her. It had been too long since she'd stood unclothed underneath a full moon, the silver light bathing her skin. She made a mental promise to herself to do it more often.

Naked, Mei, Card and Jayce stepped into the circle, holding hands that Con had tied with straps made of willow. Mei felt the tingle of magic ride her spine as she knelt on the bare earth, cool and hard beneath her knees. Jayce closed the circle then and Mei felt the protection of that wall surround them. The echoes of magic performed there in the past moved through them like a gentle tide.

As a unit they reached for the cutting blade resting in the center of the circle. Step by step they made a small cut on the arm of each person and let the blood drops touch the ground. Each patter of the blood on the ground sent a pulse of energy through the magic in the circle that reverberated through Mei's heart.

"You start, *a thaisce.*" Jayce winked.

Mei took a deep breath and centered herself. "As we will it so it shall be, we three are one as the one is three. So mote it be," Mei said softly, using the magic she'd learned from Carl and his mages. Soon the shock of intent sparked within the circle, the spell building and taking hold.

"As one is three, three is one, our power united, thy will is done," Jayce intoned, putting his Fae magic into the mix.

When Card spoke, it was in the guttural language of the Were. They'd decided against using the demon magic as it was also earth based like Jayce and Mei's.. At his last word they leaned in and kissed as a bloom of hot magic burst from them and filled the circle, looking for an escape. Finding none, it pressed back into them to the brim, until it was nearly too much, flowing through them until they could take no more and suddenly it subsided and Mei could breathe again.

Jayce's eyes widened. "I don't know about you two, but damn if I don't feel like a superhero right now."

Card laughed. "Yes, I can feel the power in my veins like lightning."

Mei nodded, unable to speak in her relief. Xethan would never take her again. She'd have the power to let go if she couldn't kill him first. A huge weight fell from her shoulders.

Jayce turned to her, taking her chin in his fingers. "You will not. Don't even think it, Mei. You will not give up or let go. As long as I have breath I will come for you. Understand? Card and I will come for you and there'll be nothing but living. We have plans, you won't mess them up by getting yourself killed."

Mei smiled up into his face. "Ah and I see the bond is stronger after the spell. You'll need to understand, Jayce, that I won't be a victim like that again. I... Something in me died, a little bit each day. And there were so many days. If it happened again I don't know that I could resist turning into something not entirely right."

"Then you'll not get taken. You'll," Jayce shook his head, "*we'll* kill him first."

Mei nodded and accepted the soft brush of his lips over hers as they stood in unison and broke the ties before stepping out of the circle and magicking themselves clothed again.

"Wow, that was some light show. I take it the spell worked?" Em asked.

"I sure hope so," Mei answered.

"I'm still working on the exact importance of midsummer. From what I can see it's pointing to solstice but I want to be absolutely sure. I'm heading back to Aine's library to research the importance of the dates to the Fae too. You don't know anything about this? It seems odd to me that so many Fae don't seem to understand the history of their magic."

Mei shrugged. "We're born with it. It just is. And most of us don't go about doing spells or even battling magicks like this. We've had our wars, we have our magic scholars but as to the more historical and arcane aspects of Fae magic, it's just not something I think about or even was educated on. Maybe when this is over you could teach the younger Fae about this kind of stuff."

"That's a very good idea, *mo fiach*," Con said to his wife, using his nickname for her.

"Ah yes, her hair is very much like the dark of a raven's wing," Mei said to her brother.

"Thank you so much, Em. We appreciate your help on this," Jayce said.

"Of course. This is end of the world stuff. We're charged with protecting the innocent and, well, I have a personal reason for wanting to stop these jerks." A fierce light came into Em's eyes.

*   *   *   *   *

Jayce sought Aine out to brief her on the spell while Card insisted Mei go and rest. Between sifting and moving about, they'd been awake for sixteen hours and he saw the exhaustion on her face.

"Are you all right, angel?" Card massaged her shoulders as she leaned into him. He loved the way she felt there, his hands on her, the scent of her skin rising to his senses like home. He knew the fact that Jayce hadn't spoken of her was bothering her.

"I'm tired. That spell was incredible but it used a lot of energy."

"Evading me, Mei? We both know you can't for very long. Just talk about it."

She heaved a sigh right as Jayce walked in.

He came to kneel next to her. "*A thaisce*? What is it? You've been unsettled all night. I can feel it even more clearly now."

Mei waved that away. "I'm fine. Really."

"I thought you said you were going to share with me." Jayce looked at her, jaw set in a firm line.

She sighed. She had said that. "I suppose it just stings to hear that your closest friends never heard of me before."

She saw the confusion turn to understanding as his anger softened. "Oh, oh *a thaisce*, it's not that I was ashamed or hiding you. I couldn't. I just couldn't. I only spoke of you with your mother and Con. It hurt too much. I felt the hole in my heart every day. But saying your name, talking about you, brought home just how empty my life had become. I didn't have someone like you had Card. I didn't have someone to share your memory with like that."

"Yes, well it wasn't a picnic having my wife's dead husband stand between us either," Card murmured and Mei turned, leaning into him a moment.

She let out her breath and looked at him. "There's so much we don't know about each other. I'm sorry all this hurts you."

He pulled her into his arms. "Mei, nothing hurt more than you being dead to me. We can muddle through, work it through. I knew you when you didn't have so much suffering, you were younger and lighter of heart. There are moments when I catch a glimpse of that girl. I fell in love with her." He caressed her cheek. "But the woman you are now, complicated, wounded, strong—that woman holds my heart and my future. It's not going to be easygoing for a while as we get to know each other again. But I'm committed to you, never, ever doubt that."

She smiled wanly. "I don't. Not really. I'm sorry I can't be that woman anymore."

"I'm sorry too, not because I don't find you fascinating and alluring and damned sexy. But because so much pain made you this way. I would magic those years in Carthau away for you if I could." Jayce kissed her temple.

"Let's talk no more of that. I wouldn't wish that time on anyone but Eire and maybe not even her. What did my mother say about the spell and the Weres as our allies?"

"She's grateful to the Weres and is talking of making Card an envoy should he want the position. She's disturbed, naturally, to hear about the situation in Sh'har and intrigued about the midsummer stuff and set some of her best scholars to work on it. She also bade me to make you rest and stay still for at least one or two days. She gave me that frown when I mentioned you were tired and had come back here to rest. I had to assure her you weren't tired on my account." Jayce winked.

"Well, you could change that. I'm certainly amenable." Mei fluttered her lashes and Card laughed.

"You're to sleep, Mei. And then we'll both be happy to tire you out. But for now, off to bed with you. I need my rest, you're insatiable. We all need the rest if Jayce and I are to keep up with your relentless lust."

Chapter Eight

∞

Indeed they did spend the next two days resting. Napping and reading when they were awake. Sparring and working on defensive magic.

Mei spent some much needed time with her mother, getting to know her again after being without her for so long.

"I've missed you so much." Aine kissed the top of Mei's head as she walked into the room and sat beside her on a couch.

"Me too. Tila, that's Card's mother, she's been the closest thing I've had to a mother for the last two thousand years. And she loves me and I her. But there's nothing like your own mother to make you feel safe and special."

Sighing, Aine put an arm around Mei's shoulders and the two leaned into each other. "I'd like to meet her, thank her for helping you through a very rough time when I wasn't there for you."

"You didn't know. Mother, you have to let go of your guilt over it. I don't blame you. Your own sister lied to you. Many, many Fae died that day at Sareem. Jayce saw me in the middle of a throng of Dark Fae before he was injured and removed. There was no reason to believe I'd been taken and Eire would lie to you about it."

"I should have known. I'm your mother. I'm the queen! What good does all my power do me if I didn't even know you were alive?"

"Oh piffle! Mother, this guilt does no one any good at all. It holds you back, it holds me back. It doesn't turn back time. All we can do is move forward. We have a job to do, we've got to stop the Dark Fae and these damnable rifts before it's too late."

"Well, I'll let go of useless guilt if you will, Mei, darling."

"What do you mean?"

"Now who gets to say piffle? You know very well what I mean. I know you feel guilt about being taken prisoner, about what those butchers did to you in Carthau. You think that guilt does you any good?"

"I do as a matter of fact." Mei moved so she could look into her mother's face.

Aine crossed her arms over her chest and gave her best queenly frown. "Is that so? Do tell."

"I'll never be taken alive again. Or if I am, I'll either break free or let go because I'll not live like that. It's a reminder of what is truly important. Life is more than just breathing in and out. A life like that is not what I wish to experience again."

Aine nodded. "It seems to me, Mei, that you could have the benefit of a cautionary tale without the guilt. Use the experience of your time at Carthau as that reminder, not baseless guilt. What happened to you was not your fault and feeling guilt over it won't erase what happened or even stop it from happening again. The guilt isn't what has made you harder. Guilt only weakens you. If you must take responsibility for what happened to you then do so and move forward. Own it and let it go. It does you no good any other way."

"It must get old."

"What's that, darling?"

"Being all wise and stuff."

Aine threw her head back and laughed, the sound filling the air with her joy. "Not yet it hasn't. I quite like the wise part. It comes after millennia of mistakes, yes? What I did with Nessa was wrong. I know that. He was married and even though I loved him more than most anything, he wasn't mine. But from that one afternoon came you. The best thing in my life. I can't be sorry for that even as I know the method was wrong. I've owned my guilt and I'm quite relieved you won't be telling Titania because even if I don't like her, I don't want her hurt. But I've owned my guilt. It was a mistake. A big one, but it's over and I can't take it back and even if I could I wouldn't. Because of you. One day you'll understand, when you have your own children."

With a deep sigh, Mei told her mother about the results of the assaults in Carthau. White-lipped with rage, Aine hugged her tight.

"Well, in the first place, Jayce is right, you can adopt. If you want to be a mother, there are other ways. Doesn't matter how the child comes into your family, it's the child that's the point. In the second place, if I ever see this Xethan myself I'll kill him. And lastly, you amaze me with your strength. You'll make a formidable queen one day."

Choking back tears, she leaned into her mother again.

* * * * *

Jayce came into the room and stood there, watching Mei as she looked out the windows over the expansive gardens. So beautiful, his woman. Complicated, exasperating, strong, courageous and irascible. Intractable even. But he'd give his last breath for her. He loved her so much that his chest ached with the fullness of it.

He knew they had to deal with this threat. It was her job, his, Card's. Their destiny and fate. But he hated it beyond bearing that she had to risk herself. It seemed a whole lot of unfair that a woman who'd suffered so much couldn't just take a holiday and leave the world saving to others.

"I can feel you," she murmured without turning to face him. "Not just your emotions, although I can feel those loud and clear. But your physical presence. I can almost feel the beat of your heart. I loved you before, of course. So much. With that bloom of youth and the certainty of absolute invincibility. I was shocked when they told me you'd died. I didn't believe it for the longest time. The belief that you'd be waiting for me when I got back to Tir na nOg was all that got me through many a day. Years. Centuries. I can still remember Eire's face when she told me you'd died in your first year at Carthau. My ears began to ring. Funny." She sighed. "And then they sent me away and I had nothing. No one. But your memory has always been here."

In the reflection of the window glass he saw her press the heel of her hand to her chest, over her heart.

"But now I see you, older and wiser, more hardened by life, and I realize that my love for you now is a million times that of the young Fae I was when we left for Sareem that day. I look at you, a man, battle-tough and yet still so good inside, and I count my blessings. I know it's hard for you, not knowing everything. I know it's hard when you see that Card knows more about those years. I'm sorry for that. I want to be more open with you because you're so important to me. I want you to know you can ask me things. I can't promise I'll be able to talk about them right when you ask but I'll do my very best to be open with you. I don't want you hurt."

A sob caught in her throat and he felt it tighten his gut. With purpose, he strode to her, his clothes falling away as he reached her.

One touch of his fingertips against her shoulder and hers disappeared as well, leaving her nude, the sun streaming through the glass making her skin look dusted with gold.

"You're a miracle to me, Mei," he murmured as his lips brushed over her neck. "The first time was amazing enough but to have you back now, after all you've endured — it's a gift I simply can't stop thanking the heavens for."

She moved to turn but he held her, her back to his front.

"I love the way your nipples look when they're hard for me. Dark pink and begging for my touch." Gently, he pushed her toward the glass until her nipples just touched the surface. He saw her reflection catch her bottom lip between her teeth.

His hands slid over the warmth of her flesh, taut and strong but also soft where a woman should be. She leaned into him, arching like a cat into his touch. Her response soothed him as much as it turned him on.

He felt her rising desire, the anticipation of what he'd do next. The spell they'd done the day before had made their emotional link far stronger. In the back of his mind he suspected it would be a plus when they finally faced Lorcan and Xethan.

"Oh so lovely. Your body is strong, sensual. The sight of you between me and Card takes my breath away. Put your hands on the window."

Slowly she raised her arms, placing her palms against the glass.

"I wonder if anyone can see up here? Do you think so, Mei? Do you think any of the people walking through the gardens is looking up at your body? Breasts high and full, my hands all over you. One sliding down to the slick lips of your pussy while the other tests the weight of your breast, thumb moving up to flick over your juicy nipple?"

There were people down there, walking, playing, not having to save the damned world. He wanted someone to look up and see him with this magnificent woman. Wanted them to know she was his.

She gasped as the tips of his fingers rode over the wet, plump labia and dipped into the well of her pussy, tickling over her distended clit.

"So ready for me. Is it that you like being watched? I remember Card talking about fucking you in an alley against a wall. Hmm. I'll have to keep that in mind the next time we all go out and we're not tracking demons or Dark Fae. I'll take you hard and fast, swallowing your cries of pleasure as people walk past, most not even noticing. But one or two might.

Might stop to watch, cock hardening. I think we may have to explore this idea, yes I do."

"You talk too much," she gasped out.

He chuckled and caught her earlobe between his teeth a moment. "Little liar. You like my talk. Your pussy is wet and swollen."

Quickly he grabbed her hips and took a step back, making her body bend forward more deeply.

"I need you now, Mei. I can't be slow. Later, I promise."

"I want it hard. I want it fast. I want it now."

He obliged, spreading her with his fingers before plunging deep in one thrust. He watched her breasts sway as he pushed into her over and over, caught the depth of longing and desire in her eyes as they met his in the window. The curve of her back was so innately feminine, even with the scars from the cat-o'-nine-tails with cold iron tips they'd used. Hatred for Xethan warred with his need for her.

"No, stop thinking of it," she gasped out and he leaned down and kissed over the scars.

The pull and clasp of her cunt, the heat of her, scalding hot, drove him, beat at him and he knew he wouldn't be long. Watching his hand slide around from her hip, he moved to her clit, felt the flutter of her inner walls as he pressed the pad of his middle finger down and then side to side. He increased the pressure and speed on her clit as he drove into her cunt with the same rhythm.

Her eyes slid closed and he saw her fingers tense against the glass, felt her pussy tighten and ready for climax around his cock and when she broke, when orgasm hit her full force, he saw the flush move up her back, felt the contractions and heard the low moan slip from her lips as she pulled him into his own climax right behind hers.

"I love you now, Mei. I loved you then. In four thousand years I've never *not* loved you." His lips pressed against the fluttering pulse at her throat as he helped her to stand straight and led her toward the bathroom.

"You're good, Jayce MacTavish. That's what got you laid the first time. If I recall, you complimented my singing voice and the color of my hair. I watched you, wanted you and you charmed your way right between my thighs."

He laughed. "Thank the gods for charm."

* * * * *

"You know, I was thinking that I should try to track the rift spots. I mean, I can seem to feel them when I'm in the area. Let's go back to the rift spot I got partially closed so I can get a scent or whatever. And then I'll work to see if I can't craft some sort of way to find them elsewhere. Also, we can see if I can't close that rift now that we've got our spiffy new powers." Mei sat at the briefing table between Card and Jayce.

"That's not a bad idea." Jayce nodded. "Em has something on the midsummer thing and perhaps she can help with the tracking magic."

"Are they coming to the briefing this morning?" Mei asked before taking a sip of coffee.

"They should be. Titania is here to sit with Elise in Con and Em's quarters." Aine's lip curled just slightly. The animus between the two Fae females was legendary but Mei knew it hurt her mother all the more because Aine knew she'd made her own trouble with Nessa first and then again later on.

"Ah, here they are," Jayce said with a welcoming wave as Con and Em entered the room, bowing to Aine before joining them.

"And how is that gorgeous little girl?" Mei asked with a grin. She'd come to have a big soft spot for her precocious niece.

"Spoiled. Spoiled and spoiled again. I'll have you know she demanded to see you when she woke up this morning..

My mother is with her now though, soothing her outrage with all manner of things Elise doesn't need."

Mei rolled her eyes at Con. "Oh yes, I'm sure she gets nothing but the strictest of rules at home."

Em laughed. "I've got something for you. I'll wait until it's my turn on the agenda."

"We've just decided it would be a good idea for Mei to go to the rift site we discovered here to see if she can't figure out some manner of magic to track them elsewhere," Card said. "I'm an excellent tracker if I do say so myself. But demon and Were magic are not like Fae magic at all. Em, we may need you to help out if it's not something Mei can automatically get a handle on."

"Well, tracking is something more easily relayed. In which case I'd appreciate it, Card, if you'd share some of your knowledge with me," Con said.

"Of course. Although from what I'm given to understand from all the young Favored, you and Jayce are quite good trackers in your own right."

Con shrugged. "Good enough, sure. But better is something to strive for, isn't it? And your skills are legendary. I keep running into people who, when I say your name, go all reverent."

A burst of pride bloomed through Mei. Card was good and he just did his job quietly, without fanfare. It was as if he had no idea how many younger trackers worshipped his skills. His humility always touched her.

Card turned to Mei and cocked his head. "Thank you for that, angel. You've no idea what it means to me."

She winked. "That new spell has invited you right into my head."

Taking her hand, he kissed her knuckles. "Indeed. An interesting place, your brain." He turned back to the others. "I'm flattered you'd ask, Con, and I'm always happy to share what I know."

"Okay, so this is what I've gathered about the midsummer reference. I've worked with some of Aine's Fae scholars and we've scoured the old texts and, combined with some of the texts I had in my library, we've figured out what the Dark Fae meant.. Because the magic of rifts opens up a space between universes, those universes must be aligned. But there are countless universes so it's not like it's an everyday occurrence to see that. In truth, it's only from late Earth spring, starting in mid-April, until midsummer, about August twentieth or so. After that the universes won't be properly set to rift until it's April on Earth again."

"Interesting. But the time slip?"

"Exactly. My guess is that Earth is probably one of the cornerstone universes and so her time is the marker the Dark Fae have to use. Which means they have to stay on Earth to keep the Dark Fae elsewhere apprised of when they can use rifts again." Em sat back in her chair.

"Wow. Well, that gives them what? What was the month when you left?" Jayce asked.

"It's early July. But you know how that goes. A day here can be months there or just a few hours. So I've had a sentry set up in our house in New Orleans to alert us once it gets to be August first," Con explained.

"Well, let's get to work then." Mei stood. "I want to get to the rift site as soon as possible. See if I can track and close them. I'm very concerned with the matter streams leaking. I'd like to speak to the Donovan about that as well. See if we can't get any more information out of him about what's happening in the other universes."

"You go on to the rift site. I'll summon Carl," Aine said.

"Have you forgiven him?" Jayce asked Mei.

"I don't know. That's a lot to forgive. But I'll take his help, that's for damned sure. Shall we go?"

* * * * *

In the blink of an eye Jayce, Card, Mei, Con and Em all stood at the rift site in Tir na nOg.

It was still there, the jagged rip in space-time. Still leaking a stream of matter from another world into their own. The air there felt inherently wrong. Thin.

Mei walked to the rift and studied it carefully.

"Can you see it? Or just sense it?" Em asked.

"At first, when we were here before, I could sense it. But now? I can see the matter out of the corner of my eye. Like dust motes. I can feel it, like air coming through a cracked window. It's wrong here. Can you feel it?"

Em nodded. "I can. It feels less solid than the universe feels at the palace or our house by the sea. Like it's flickering."

"I think it's the damage. The matter working to destabilize existence here. The longer it's open the worse it will become. Many spots like this all over the universes will make the deterioration worse. That much I can feel in my bones." It troubled Mei, the reality of what could happen. She had to fix it.

"That makes sense. We should work on two things. First, can you focus in? See what makes it different? Perhaps you can find a way to grab hold of that so you can look for it to track. And then you need to close this rift and every one you find. Stop the bleed of matter."

"Smart woman." Mei closed her eyes and let the data wash through her. Thought about what made it different from the surrounding space, grabbed hold of that and mulled it over. It had a scent almost. A signature.

Like a key, she placed it into her arsenal of magic and contemplated how she'd work to find the right lock to use it in. How she'd apply what she'd learned to track more rifts elsewhere.

"Okay, I have it. I'm just not quite sure how to use it to track."

Em squatted next to her. "Can you show me? Link with me and show me what that signature looks like?"

They held hands and Mei let Em into her head to see the pattern. Mei felt the subtle brush of Em's entry, slow and sure. Felt Em's slow examination of everything Mei had seen of the rift.

And some long minutes later, felt Em's retreat.

"Wow, you think in fractals."

"Fractals?"

"Chaos theory. A mathematical theory about the foundations of the universe. Very complicated math that makes the most beautiful patterns called fractals. I've never seen another person who thinks in that way. Other than me, anyway," Em said.

Mei shrugged. "Well, I suppose I believe that everything is math in a sense. And the magic I was born with isn't my only magic. The warriors taught me witch and wizard magic and I learned some Were magic as well. It just all comes to me as numbers when I think about it."

"Me too." Em smiled. "That's really cool. I think you and I can work some magic together here. If all the universes are data, you simply need to isolate the data the rifts create. You seek it out and you should be able to track it that way. Perhaps not through all the universes from here, but I think these spots where the rifts are, are conduits somehow. They may amplify the way to the next spot. If you'll link with me again I'll show you what I mean about a locator spell."

"Makes sense. Okay, I'm game."

"This isn't going to send her off somewhere, is it? I don't want her tearing off alone," Card asked and Jayce let out his breath, nodding.

"No. I'm just going to help her channel her magic to forge a tracking spell."

Mei smiled up at her men before turning back to Em and letting her link again.

Jayce watched as the two women knelt face-to-face, eyes closed, for close to half an hour. The air was thick with magic. He recognized Mei's—a mixture of three magical pathways, spicy, seductive. Em's was lighter but strong. He realized they were also making a new kind of magic together and that had its own unique feel as well.

After a time both women opened their eyes and sat back on their heels.

"Wow. Em, you're a genius. I had no idea I could use my magic like that. I also think you showed me a way to close the rift." Mei stood and Con helped Em up.

"I did?" Em blushed.

"Yes," Mei said absently as she walked toward the rift. "I've been thinking of it wrong. Like using glue to attach the two sides back together. But that leaves a weak spot. And it's not what will work. Hang on, I'm going to try something."

She closed her eyes again and reached toward the rift. Instead of trying to pull the two halves closed, she re-envisioned the spot as one whole. Essentially rewriting the code of the rift's existence and programming it out.

When she opened her eyes the world swayed a bit and Card reached out to catch her in his arms.

"You did it," Em said. "It feels clean here, more solid. There's still a smudge from the matter leak but that wavering in the air is gone."

"I did. I was approaching it wrong. It wasn't a matter of pulling two halves together but re-imagining the rift as one whole spot in space-time. Essentially magicking the world back into one piece and unraveling the rift so there were no longer two halves but one whole. The math thing we talked about did it. I was looking at it backward."

"Mei, don't talk about it like it was no big deal. I couldn't even see the rift until you pointed it out. I'd have walked right past. Probably felt something wrong, but not been able to really get a bead on it."

"I think the spell you made for us in New Orleans and the work you and I just did helped me a lot. And rift magic is apparently in my maternal line. All things that I suppose were meant to happen so we could end this." Mei shrugged tiredly. "But I will say it takes a lot out of you, to re-imagine the universe whole where it was ripped."

"You're very pale. Let's get you back home for a bit. Get some food into you. We need to talk to the Donovan anyway. You can work on the tracking spell once you're rested. You should be fresh for that, especially if you're going to close them as we find them." Jayce nuzzled her temple. "I'm so proud of you."

They stood once more in the palace gardens before heading inside. Mei took a deep breath, letting the scent of the flowers relax her. They had a solution to part of the problem but the biggest problem was the Dark Fae and that wasn't so easily solved.

"I can hear the wheels turning in there," Card murmured as they approached Aine's rooms.

"Just thinking about the scope of this problem."

"We've tried peace talks, look where they've gotten us," Con said. "They've attempted to kill me and mine and make no mistake, Mei NiaAine, you're mine too. We've beaten them and tried to welcome them back into our society and all we've gotten is more scheming. They can't be allowed to continue to exist."

Mei sighed as she heaved onto a couch. Card and Jayce settled on either side while Con and Em snuggled into a large chair across from them. Her mother's secretary ran off to fetch her. In the meantime, Jayce created a table full of food and drinks.

"You need it. Go on." He nudged Mei, who leaned over to fill her plate, and Card handed her a glass of juice. Everyone else began to eat, each lost in thought until Aine entered with the Donovan.

"Mei, you're so pale. Are you all right?" Aine moved to Mei, feeling her forehead, looking concerned.

"She closed the rift, stopped the matter leak," Jayce said.

"You did? Excellent. Mei, darling, I'm very proud of you."

"I knew you could, sweetpea."

Mei looked up into the Donovan's face. A face she'd often thought of as fatherly. Still it was hard to shake the feeling of betrayal. He'd known all along that she hadn't been exiled by her mother. Known that Jayce wasn't dead. And yet he'd said nothing for years while she suffered and grieved. He'd told her mother things about Mei's time in Carthau without her permission.

"Mei, will you take a walk with me?" the Donovan asked.

"No, I don't want her up and around. We'll all give you some space while I update Aine on what we did this morning," Jayce said as he stood. The others followed suit and left as the Donovan sat across from her, studying her face.

"You're angry with me."

"No. Ya think?"

He chuckled. "Sarcasm, tsk tsk. I wanted to tell you. You must believe me. But I was forbidden to. Then when you and Card... Well, what could I do then? You loved him, he loved you. You'd both healed each other. And I still couldn't tell you. I am sorry. I never wanted to have you without your mother for so long. It tore both of you apart and Jayce as well, lost without you. But as you're aware I'm bound by a set of rules, much as you are. My rules are set into my contract by blood oath. When I say I wanted to tell you and I couldn't, I meant I physically couldn't. I love you like my own child in many ways. I'd never want to hurt you on purpose."

"You told my mother all that stuff about my injuries and The Bona Dea! It tore her up, made her feel worse than she already did. That happened to me, it was mine to share or not.

You had no right." Mei's hands balled into fists at the memory of her mother's face that morning.

"Sweetpea, you may have guessed that your mother and I are familiar with each other?"

Mei wrinkled her nose. "Ew, too much information, Carl!"

"At last you call me Carl. Two millennia I've been asking and now you finally do it."

"I should call you The Messenger just to annoy you."

"Ah, that's an old one. Where'd you hear that one?"

Mei told him about the things they'd overheard in Sh'mura at the palace.

"Interesting. Obviously your aunt saw me here and told them of my involvement. She's a wretched bitch."

Mei waved a hand in the air. "We've established that. So you and my mother are, uh, friendly. How long?"

"The last five hundred years or so. I tried to hint around about Eire and even you but as I said, what I could reveal was limited. But she was hurting, Mei. She needed to know. Sometimes a parent needs that. What she was imagining wasn't as bad as reality. It was the not knowing that was so painful. I couldn't do that to her, or to you. I didn't want you to have to tell her all of that. It was hard enough watching you endure it. I hated the idea of you reliving it. So she asked me, desperate to know, and I told her what I could and up to the limits of what I felt you could forgive."

"It's difficult, having her know. Having anyone know."

"Mei, you've lived through more than most do. And you've done it with such strength and courage that I'm consistently amazed. But you take too much on yourself. Let others share your load and stop blaming yourself for what is purely on the shoulders of others. And you should forgive me because I'm cute and I love you and I need you as one of my warriors."

Heaving a sigh, Mei rolled her eyes. "Perhaps after a long vacation, when this is over, I can see my way fit to forgiving you. In the meantime, what can you tell me about the rift spots in the other universes? I've closed one here and I'm going to go out and use a spell to find and close the others as I go. But I need to know—how long have they been rifting? We know they can only open rifts at certain times of the year. But if this has been going on for years I'd like to see if I can deal with the oldest rifts first. Get those closed up."

"From our intelligence, it's just been this cycle. They've been working on the spell for hundreds of years but none of them has had the gift. But recently they recruited a Fae to their side who had part of the gift. The reason the spells are so haphazard is because they're using three and four Fae to do it. Their magic doesn't meld together totally, which makes the rift even more unstable. We don't know who they recruited though, I can see the question on your face."

She nodded. "We've asked Brian and the others but the Dark Fae have been smart enough to run in small cells instead of a big network. Not a whole lot of people knew what was going on other than with their own group. Effective."

"Yes. I can offer you some of our people to go with you when you head to the rift sites. You'll need the backup. Before long you'll be bound to run into some Dark Ones."

"Thank you. May I choose?"

Donovan inclined his head a moment in agreement.

"I'd like Ashe, Kai, Rasa and Bedwin."

"Done. I'll send them to you immediately. Excellent choice. I think when this is over you and I need to talk about advancement."

Mei fought a grin. "Thank you, Carl. And you'll seek me out if you hear anything?"

"Yes and the same goes for you. We've put some of our people on Earth to watch the time slip. I'll coordinate with them and you on that."

"Okay. Con's put some people on it as well, but having another set of eyes won't harm anything."

"Indeed." Carl stood and held his hands out. She followed and moved to him, taking his hands in her own. "Thank you for your forgiveness. I will see you soon. I'll send the others to the gardens."

"You're welcome. But let's have them meet me at the rift site. Why don't you stay and see if I can't find the next one and then have them sent there? It makes more sense than bringing them here and having to sift everyone elsewhere."

"Good idea. Let's do that then."

"It's very shielded in here. Let's get away from the palace to see if I can't get a better lock."

She quickly notified the relevant people of her intentions and then shimmered to a field just south of the palace complex.

"Con, I'd like you to stay here with my mother and Em," Mei said as she got settled, sitting on the cool earth.

"Mei, I'm one of the best warriors you've got. I can't stay behind when I could help."

"Con, she's right. Aine needs the best and you shouldn't leave Em and the babe. I need a man I can trust here, you need that too." Jayce squeezed Con's shoulder.

Con snorted. "Fine. But I swear, someone had better twist some heads for me."

Chuckling, Mei closed her eyes and sent her magic out like a beacon, looking for that cluster of numbers and patterns that marked a rift. What she hadn't expected was to see so many of them. She chose the one she saw leaking the most matter, got a lock and stood.

"Got it. There are a lot of them. We're going to close as many as we can, keeping as quiet as we can. I don't want to alert them any quicker than we have to on this." She told Carl where the first rift point was and the next three they'd travel to as well and he assured her he'd send the other warriors there to meet her. In the blink of an eye he was gone.

Everyone filed back but Aine. "Be safe, darling, or I will be very cross."

Mei smiled. "Gotcha. Now you all get back to the palace. I want you safe."

"Well, let's go. I've felt itchy for a fight for weeks now," Card growled and Jayce laughed, patting the hilt of his sword.

Mei suited up, knife sheaths on each wrist and a 10 mm Glock 20 on each thigh in a holster. Her clothes were specially created to repel bullets, magic and knife and sword edges. She took a look at Card and nodded, seeing he'd put his on, and with a quick burst of magic Jayce was wearing them too.

"Uh, thank you, *a thaisce*. Nice weapons."

"I don't waste time with swords if I can shoot. I'm not that agile with a blade but I'm a crack shot. Shall we go?"

When they answered in the affirmative they sifted away from Tir na nOg and to a high vista in Aurelia. She'd opted for a concealment spell but was relieved that no one else was in the immediate area.

"The others should be here shortly. Jayce, set up a concealment spell around this area, I won't be able to work with one around me personally."

He nodded and moved to obey, finishing just as the first one of the warriors appeared. They weren't Fae, they didn't have the same kind of sifting power, but each had powers of intra-universe transport.

Kai, the nearly eight-foot-tall warrior from Alandria, crouched, scanning the area.. He was the third son in a world where none mattered but the heir and the second son. His father the king had sent him to Carl when the boy was just eight years old.

He caught sight of Mei and Card and smiled. "Greetings! I see you've started the party without me." He swooped in and pulled Mei off the ground and into a hug. Jayce looked

Lauren Dane

askance but Card didn't seem alarmed so he kept his cool. He didn't have to like the man holding his woman but he was glad to see her held in high esteem by her peers.

Kai gently put her to her feet and Mei straightened her clothes before turning to those gathered there. "This is Kai, he's a real hand with a battle axe and a crossbow. Kai, this is my other husband, Jayce MacTavish, the Queen's Left Hand."

Kai's eyebrows rose. "Donovan's people told us about the lies that have been told. I wanted to kill someone on your behalf." The murderous look on his face cheered her. Kai turned to Jayce. "I'm pleased to know you."

By that time, in popped Rasa, the leonine shifter with the gorgeous golden eyes and a mane of amber-colored hair around his very handsome face. Rasa had been abandoned by his Pride when he was an infant, left exposed to die because of the mark on his side they'd decided made him a demon.

It was a beautiful white spot and Rasa was the furthest thing from a demon Mei had ever known. He was also lightning quick, utterly merciless on a battlefield and an amazing tactician.

He bowed and spoke in his growly bass voice. "Mei and Card, good to see you. Kai, you as well." He nodded and turned to Jayce, whom Mei introduced. He hesitated a moment but once he looked to Card, who grinned and nodded, he shook Jayce's hand. Mei scowled but Jayce waved it away.

Ashe was a human mage who'd grown up in Rome. He'd been raised by one of the Donovan's human assistants and brought into the ranks of the warriors when he turned twenty-one. That had been a thousand years ago. Mei didn't ask how he remained alive so long. His power was a palpable thing and she just assumed it was due to that. In any case the tall, lithe man with the raven hair sprinkled with gray at the temples turned his light blue eyes her way and winked.

Card groaned and they all started to laugh. "Okay, okay. Card, will you introduce Jayce to Ashe and Bed when she

154

shows up? I want to get started on this rift. I want to get out of here as soon as possible."

Card chuckled and nodded, handling the introductions, which settled into background noise, and she approached the rift. It wasn't a large one, it hadn't even been opened all the way. But the work was sloppy and matter rushed through. Settling back into herself, confident that she'd be protected while doing the magic, she reached out and saw the rift through her third eye. Slowly, methodically, she knit the world back into one piece as she envisioned it whole instead of torn.

When she came back to herself she heard Bedwin's musical voice speaking lowly.

"It's done," Mei said, turning to them all. Bed stood there in her usual Stevie Nicks outfit, all gauzy and witchy-looking. Pretty brown eyes, full pouty lips, porcelain skin and a body that made men and women stop and stare—Bed was a total package. She was also a mixture of bloodthirsty species—part Sh'hari, part vampire and a bit of demon. The demon part enabled her to be out during the day. Normally someone with her pedigree would be as evil as they come but as an infant she'd been rescued from a village raid by Ashe. He'd taken her in and become her father figure and she'd become a warrior some two hundred years prior.

"Nice to see you, Mei." Bedwin waved and Mei blew her a kiss.

"You okay, angel?" Card asked.

"Tired, but we have work to do. Let's get the hell out of here before we get noticed."

"Let's motor then, shall we?" Ashe held his hand out and they all grasped each other and sifted to the next rift spot. And the one after that. And another, this one on Earth.

"Set the perimeter while I do this one."

"And then we're off to the Ritz for a hearty meal and sleep. You look like hell, Mei." The look on Card's face

155

brooked no argument, especially when Mei saw it echoed on every other face there in that forest glade.

"Fine." She turned and focused in, pulling the magic from within her, from the ground at her feet and the air around her and using it to put the spot to rights again.

When she finished it was far past dark. The stars blinked in the night sky. The scent of the sun-warmed bark on the trees rose along with that of the loam of the forest floor.

"Feels much better."

The smile on her face faded as she saw movement in the shadows. Saw the glow of eyes. "Fuck! We're not alone," she yelled out as she shoved Jayce to the dirt, riding his body down as she unholstered her weapon and fired.

At the sound of the howl, a feral grin broke over her face. "Die, asshole."

The glade was suddenly alive with movement as Dark Fae and demons flooded it, weapons drawn. Mei didn't have much magic left after closing the rifts but she did have enough energy to kick some ass.

Handguns in both hands, she took her time and picked off her foes one by one as she waded around the action, careful not to hit any of their people. Card had shifted partially and was ripping the other demons apart with his bare hands. The gleam of Kai's axe was visible in the moonlight, Ashe's magic crackled against his Dark Fae opponents and Jayce was a sight to behold as he worked that giant sword, clashing with two Dark Fae who were clearly outmatched. Bed's knives were wicked as she moved lightning quick among the group.

Mei found herself hauled around to face a demon. He held her arms down so she was unable to shoot him. A look at his face told her this demon was one of her torturers at Carthau. Rage so deep she didn't even know it had simmered within her boiled up. A jerk of her head forward connected her forehead just right and she showed her teeth as a sickening crunch sounded and the warmth of his blood painted her upper body. Still he held on but unluckily for him there were a few things in common between humans and demons. One of them was that it hurt like a mother when a woman kneed a male demon in his nutsac. Which she did. Twice.

Letting her go with a howl of pain, he crumpled toward the ground, but she'd dispatched him before he fully hit his knees.

"I bet that felt good," Card said into her ear as he put his arm around her. "I need to clean up. Jayce, why don't you all go to the Ritz Carlton in Laguna Niguel? It's just down the coast from here. I'll be there in about an hour."

"Why are you staying? Can I help?"

Card squeezed Jayce's shoulder. "No, but thanks. I'm going to clean up. I can produce fire hot enough to melt bones. By the time I'm done here there'll be no evidence. Go on, get her some rest. Order me a Porterhouse steak, rare. I'll be there." Card kissed Mei's forehead and turned to get to work.

"I'll stay with him, just in case," Kai said. "I'm not worried, I don't think anyone else is coming but I know blondie would feel much better if we did and it looks like she's about to pass out." He also kissed Mei's forehead and she smiled weakly in his direction.

"Thank you, Kai. I do feel better. But you should just transport out. Promise me."

"I do promise you. Now go. The sooner you go, the sooner I can finish," Card called out and Jayce shimmered six hundred miles to the south along with the others..

* * * * *

Ashe held his hand out to stop them as they stood in the parking lot. "I'll get us checked in. They might call the police if they caught sight of her." He ran the same hand over his body and his clothes were fresh and clean and he was the epitome of casual money.

He was back within ten minutes, handing key cards to everyone.

"If you're all right, Mei, we'll just see you in the morning. We'll get back to work after some rest. He was one of them? The one you killed last?" Bed tucked a loose lock of Mei's hair behind her ear.

Mei could only nod..

"Good then. A bit less frustrated rage and one less demon walking the worlds. Go and rest now, you look all worn out."

With that and a promise to meet for breakfast in Mei's room at eight the next morning they all shimmered directly to their rooms.

"*A thaisce*, let's get you in the bathtub. I'll do us a nice dinner while you're soaking." Jayce gently helped her out of her clothes as the bathwater ran.

"I want room service. Trust me, Jayce, it's a wonderful experience. There'll be a book by the phone on the desk in the sitting room," she said drowsily as she stepped into the steamy water.

He watched her, concern aching in his chest. It'd been amazing fighting with her there in that glade. She'd been fearless, taking her shots not wildly but slowly and methodically. He wasn't one for handguns but he admired her skill. His heart had stopped for a moment when he'd caught sight of the demon grabbing her the way it had. Backed into a corner, locked in a swordfight with another Fae, he'd been unable to get to her. Shimmering that short a distance wasn't effective so he'd battled to get free to get to her when she'd taken the demon down and then ended its life.

But she seemed so fragile just then. The juxtaposition of her ways always startled him. Strong enough to headbutt a demon and break its nose but wounded deeply by what had happened to her in Carthau. And she'd closed five rifts that day alone without resting from the time she'd done the magic with Em back in Tir na nOg.

After consulting her he ordered room service, including Card's steak, and conjured up a bottle of whiskey and three glasses. He didn't bother with a shower and just magicked himself clean and into comfortable clothing.

She came out of the bathroom some twenty minutes later, a little more color in her face but moving slowly.

"Hey there, darlin'. You're looking a wee bit better. The food should be here shortly, I asked them to give us half an hour but here," he conjured a platter of fresh fruit and cheese, "eat a little so you can have a sip or five of some good Fae whiskey."

"Warm me up from the inside out, eh?" She laughed before nibbling on the fruit.

"Are you all right?" He wanted her to share with him, didn't want to have to beg to know her.

"Whiskey first."

He poured her two fingers and she took a bracing sip. "Hits the spot. The last one I killed was one of my torturers at Carthau. Looked like a television newscaster, you know? Perfect hair, he always had this expression on his face, even when he was hurting me, just sort of pleasantly blank. I don't know, it seemed worse that he never had any expression. Like assaulting me was no more or less important to him than tying his shoes. I hated him. He's the source of the burns. And now he's dead. I win."

He took a deep breath. "You do. Thank you for telling me, I know it couldn't have been easy."

She shrugged. "You deserve to know. I told you I'd try to share what I could when I could. It's not a pretty story. What I did wasn't pretty."

"No. But it was what you needed to do. And you can let go a bit more, aye?"

Nodding, she took another sip. "Aye, indeed."

Just after the food arrived, Card popped into the room. "Perfect timing, I see. Keep it warm for me, angel, I need a quick shower."

Mei watched his back as he headed into the bathroom and smiled. "I'm lucky to have you both. It's one thing to be listened to, it's another to be understood."

Jayce kissed her fingertips.

A few minutes later Card emerged with a puff of steam and sat with them, digging into his meal with gusto. "All clean out there. At some point I expect the rest of them to figure out what's happening. Not today, but soon. We killed them all but someone will be looking for them."

"Next time we should keep one alive to question him. Why were they there? Were they trying to open it farther? To redo the spell? Five mature demons and twenty Dark Fae don't just show up to one of a hundred rifts for no reason."

"Thought about that myself as I was working. Fine work you did there, Mei. In any case, we'll keep one of the Fae alive and take him back to the palace to have a truthseeker work on him. It'd be stupid to think we could make a demon talk. The stakes for them are worse than death at our hands if they talk," Card said with a shrug.

"How did those rounds stop the demons anyway? I thought they were impervious to stuff like bullets."

Mei smiled at Jayce. "Ah, but these bullets have a silver core and they're all spelled. Takes a lot of effort but it's worth it."

"I'm just twisted enough that your vicious side really turns me on."

Card laughed and slapped Jayce on the back. "Welcome to the club." He turned to Mei. "Angel, did you drink the tea? Your color isn't right. I knew we should have stopped after the fourth rift."

"No we shouldn't have.." Mei's voice was hard. "And no, I didn't drink the tea. I forgot." Mei sighed and moved to stand but Card waved her down.

"Sit." He moved quickly and efficiently, pulling an assortment of items from her pack. A mug, a pouch and a bottle of clear liquid. Jayce watched as Card poured the water into the mug, dropped the little pouch into it and held it between both his hands. He stood there, eyes closed, until steam began to rise from the mug and he placed it on the table and rejoined them. "You can't forget. You'll feel like hell tomorrow if you don't."

"What is that?" Jayce asked.

"It's a restorative tea. You've seen her drink it often enough," Card explained.

Mei took a deep breath. "My time in Carthau did a lot of damage to me, as I've told you. It weakened me. When I use a lot of magic I tend to feel drained physically and the next day I wake up with full body soreness and a muzzy brain. But when The Bona Dea came to help she brought this tea. The herbs are easy enough to find and put together. Card's mother makes it for me in batches so it stays fresh."

"Well, why didn't you tell me? I could have made you a cup while you were in the bath. Mei, let me help you."

"I hate it! I was so damned strong and now I'm not. I have to slow down to rest after magic now in a way I never did before. I'm weak."

Jayce moved quickly, pulling her into his lap, handing her the mug. "Drink that while I chew you out. Go on or I'll get cranky, as you like to say." He waited until she took a sip before continuing. "Now then, if you need to stop to rest we will stop. Period. I will not have you burning yourself out. As I see it, you're the only weapon we've got against these rifts. So far from being weak, you're powerful. Mei, you have got to let go of this guilt. You're lucky to be alive and you're so much more than that. You're a warrior, someone I'm proud to fight beside. Your magic is strong and hale and your courage is," he paused, looking for the right word, "unimaginable. I cannot even contemplate what you've endured but you more than endured, you *survived*. So you need to rest after using your magic. I can't do rift magic at all, does that make me weak?"

She snorted, rolling her eyes, but took another drink of the tea.

"You do no one any good when you push yourself too far. If you fry your circuits we have nothing against them to stop the rifts. So tomorrow we get up, eat breakfast and do two rifts. Rest. Do two more. Rest. Repeat. Does that work for you, Card?"

"I think that's a fine idea, Jayce. Angel?"

"I'm not made of glass, you know."

"Mei, don't get pissy for the sake of being pissy. You know he's right. It makes sense and it's the best use of your power and our energy. It also gives us time to think on what we've seen. This is more than just the rifts, we need to be thinking strategically about how to deal with the Dark Fae and the demons working with them." Card popped a piece of steak into his mouth and grinned.

"You're both insufferable bullies," she said but her voice was mild as she finished the tea. "Fine. As you'll both pout if I don't, we'll try it your way for now. The next several rifts are here and then in Sh'har let's do that tomorrow. We can stay here again tomorrow night."

"No. We need to move to a different place nightly. They're going to be tracking us," Jayce said and Card nodded.

"You're right. Okay, now that you've both bossed me around, someone needs to make me come before I go to sleep. Tomorrow I want to look at a map of these rifts. There's something nagging at the back of my mind but I can't quite get a lock on it."

Jayce stood, keeping her in his arms. "Are you sure you don't just want to go to sleep now? We can take you when you wake."

Reaching out, she smoothed the worry lines from his forehead. "I promise you, if I were too strung out I would just go to bed now. After a meal and the bath and tea I feel better. Certainly well enough to be ravished by two extremely sexy males with lovely hard cocks and making me come on their minds."

Card chuckled and pushed them both toward the bedroom. "Angel, you sure you want someone to make you come? You only mentioned that twice in the last five minutes."

"I just wanted to be sure I got it on record. You know, in case someone might have forgotten." Her last word rose as Jayce tossed her on the bed and she stared up at the two of them, looking more ferocious and handsome than any men had a right to.

They stood side by side, Jayce the taller of the two with long, thick muscle, sun-kissed skin, that fiery hair down to his waist and amethyst-blue eyes. She knew from experience the rough feel of the calluses from how he'd held his sword all the millennia he'd served the queen. The sound of his voice, that velvet of his accent, never failed to make her weak in the knees.

And Card, not quite six feet tall. All hard muscle and menace. His elemental nature as a wolf came out when he moved, graceful and terrifying all at once. His hair, a cap of messy, soft brown-blond curls, took the edge off the square line of his jaw and the suspicion in his eyes. His lips were carnally feral.

The two of them were perfectly masculine. Hard-core, ass-kicking testosterone machines. And both quite handy in the sack.

She sighed, satisfied, and both men smiled. "You do give the best non-verbal compliments, angel." Card's smile turned wicked and a shiver broke through her.

"And you know?" Jayce tapped his chin as if he were thinking. "Come to think of it, I think *you* should make yourself come first. Show us how it's done."

"Very good idea. I endorse that plan." Card reached back and pulled two chairs forward and both men sat and watched.

"You think I won't?"

"Oh I know you will. Angel, one of my favorite things in the world is watching you touch that sweet pussy. Go on now, give us a show. And then we'll join in." He sat back.

"Pillows behind you so I can see better, *a thaisce.*" Jayce waggled his brows.

Sitting, she reached around herself to pile pillows behind her back and arms, giving herself a nice platform to rest on. She planned to give them a show they'd remember. Slowly she spread her thighs, a smile crossing her lips briefly as both men made soft groans of pleasure at the sight of her pussy.

Her eyes dropped closed as she smoothed her hands over her skin softly. Her nipples tingled and began to throb as the pleasure began to pulse through her body. For long moments she drew her palms over the tips and then drew her fingers over them, tugging, then pinching and rolling.

She felt her cunt swell and get slick, clasping on itself, needing to be filled.

One hand skimmed down her belly, fingertips grazing over wet labia, avoiding her clit. Instead she pressed two deep inside herself, felt the flutter of her inner muscles..

"Are you tight?" Jayce asked.

"Yes," she gasped out.

"Wet and hot?"

She could only manage a moan in the affirmative as her thumb pressed over her clit.

"Aye, I love the way your pussy feels when it's all slick. Hot and swollen, juicy and creamy. I can see how wet you are now, Mei. Your thighs are glistening," Card murmured.

"And you're impatient. You feel your clit under your thumb, you want to come, don't you?" Jayce's voice was taut with desire.

He was right. She could never be patient when she made herself come. Orgasm was too delicious to hold back. Her head tipped back and she pressed the heel of her hand down on her clit, pressing the knuckle of her thumb over her clit and slipping another finger into herself.

Climax roared through her as a gasp tore from her mouth but before the ripples had even stopped moving through her she felt the bed dip on both sides as they joined her. Hands, one pair steaming hot, the other cool but work hard, caressed every inch of her skin.

When she opened her eyes she found herself looking at the fat head of Card's cock. Rolling over quickly, she took him into her mouth, humming at his taste. One of his hands tangled into her hair, holding her just so.

"Ass up in the air, Mei. I'm going to fuck you right now while you suck Card's cock." Jayce's strong hands helped her get into position so she didn't have to break contact with Card's cock.

She couldn't help but cry out around him though, when Jayce thrust into her in one hard move. And he didn't stop. He began to fuck into her hard and fast as she continued to go down on Card.

Within moments she was caught up in the rhythm they made, the up and down, push and pull, in and out of their sex. Mei felt not like one person within a group but one unit made of three. Drowning in sensation, helpless against the tide of emotion her men put out through their bonds, Mei simply gave in to it, let it happen and carry her.

Card's thigh muscles flexed and bunched under her palms as she balanced herself there. She knew he was close, smelled the heat rising from him. Taking a deep breath through her nose, she took him into her mouth to the back of her throat over and over until she heard his ragged groan and felt his release, tasted the spice of him.

Jayce reached around and played over her clit with his fingertips, featherlight but just right. Before long another climax hit and she pushed back into him, squirming.

"Fuck," he whispered harshly and she felt the jerk of him deep inside her cunt as he came, holding her against him tight for long moments until the two of them collapsed to the side and Card settled in next to her.

"Sleep now. We've got a big day tomorrow." Card pressed a kiss to her forehead and Jayce kissed the back of her neck before the three of them settled down together, finding comfort and warmth as their bodies lay against each other.

Chapter Nine

සා

The next morning Card awoke to the scent of coffee and an empty bed. He stretched and got up, shuffling naked out to the sitting area where Mei sat at her laptop. Her lovely hair was caught back from her face in a jade clip he'd given her a thousand years before, those long-as-sin legs encased in denim. He did like her in those tight, long-sleeved shirts she wore. He liked her in everything, he supposed with a smile.

He bent to catch a kiss as he poured himself coffee from the carafe. "Morning, angel. Feeling better today?"

"I certainly had a nice workout last night," she said absently as she stared at the screen.

"Where's Jayce?" Card took a sip before pulling on a pair of jeans.

"He popped over to New Orleans to check in with the people Con set to watch the situation. He should be back in a few minutes. The others will be here in a few minutes. Breakfast is on the way. I ordered for you."

"Thank you. You want to tell me what's got you so fascinated you aren't even giving me that look you normally do when I walk around shirtless in worn jeans?"

That got her attention. She turned to take a look, her eyes going sexy and slumberous. "Very nice. You do fill them out so well. And why do your feet look so sexy?"

He laughed. "You're good for my ego."

"Hmpf. It's true and you know it. It's not like you were a shy virgin before me. Believe me, I've faced enough of your former *friends* to know that."

He snorted and motioned back at the laptop. "Whatever. You know damned well I haven't even looked at another woman in two thousand years. So what are you looking at?"

"Well, it's been niggling at the back of my mind for a while. Ever since I first got a lock on the rifts. I can't believe it's all random, the placement."

A knock sounded and he waved her to remain seated while he went to get it. It was the others, with the room service carts right behind them.

"Just set that table up there," Card told the room service folks while Ashe, Bedwin, Kai and Rasa stood back but alert while they worked putting out the food.

After a healthy tip they all sat to eat, Mei joining them. Within moments Jayce shimmered into the room and it shifted from quiet to a buzz of conversation and planning.

Jayce explained nothing much had happened. They knew it was mid-July but the sentries would work with Con as well as Jayce to be sure they were in place on time.

"Okay, I think Mei has something to tell us," Card said, interrupting them all.

She started off by explaining her feelings that the placement of the rifts couldn't be random. "We know that dark magic is amplified by places that radiate power. We also know Fae and other light-based paths are as well. You know, standing stones, burial grounds, sacred places to generations of cultures who live and worship and perform rituals in a space."

"Sure. That makes sense. Magic is energy. Energy never disperses, it just changes to another kind of energy." Jayce shrugged and Ashe nodded.

"That's how dark magic works in general. It often pulls extra power from the earth to boost a spell. Sometimes there's death magic, which means, of course, sacrifice and blood," Ashe added.

"So it stands to reason then that sites where horrific events have happened would also be powerful for dark magic practitioners." Mei reached out and grabbed her laptop. "Using our data mapping, I've created a three-dimensional map of the rift sites."

"Angel, when did you do all this work?" Card narrowed his eyes at his wife.

"I'm fine. I woke up a few hours earlier than you two did. I had the data mapping thing in mind already and one of the Donovan's people was quite helpful and did most of the work, actually. The programming part was way beyond my ability."

Jayce made a low growling sound, which surprised Card as he was usually the growler in the room. He was pleased to see Jayce concerned about how hard Mei pushed herself too, though.

"Anyway," Mei hurried along past their scowls. "If you'll look here, you can see the sites on Earth are all clustered around sites of power." She pointed at the screen.

"Sites of great evil. Auschwitz, The Killing Fields, here at Little Big Horn and in Bataan. They're tapping the negative magics. Which leads me to believe their people don't have the same level of power I have. Carl said they had a team of people working on the rift spell instead of just one."

"If we can take a few of them out we significantly weaken their side," Rasa said.

"There's no way we can erase the stain of Auschwitz so yes, we've got to focus on getting the rifts closed to stop the matter leaks and to try to take out the people they've got who can open those rifts to begin with." Mei sat back.

"Well, it's my belief that they'll be figuring out what we're doing soon enough. And then they'll start sending teams to attack us, to defend the rifts they've already opened up. Opening new ones seems a great deal more difficult than making an existing one larger," Jayce said as he drank his juice.

"The closer we get to midsummer the more desperate they're going to be. We'll have to hit hard when we can or we'll be hit," Card said.

"Aye." Jayce nodded.

"So let's get going. Let's do a few here, rest and move to those in Sh'har." Card stood, grabbing a shirt and pulling it on. Mei rolled her eyes at Bed's stares. Bedwin shrugged.

"What? You see him naked all the time. A girl's gotta get her looking in while she can. It's not like I go home to that every night." Bedwin winked and Mei laughed.

In a flash she was outfitted again, ready for battle but not carrying anything extra. Free to move quickly and quietly. In moments the rest of the group was outfitted for battle and stealth before they sifted to the first rift of the day.

* * * * *

They came to stand in a grassy area leading to what is called "Hell's Gate" at Auschwitz.. Train tracks still lay in the ground on the left. Mei felt the energy of the place. So unsettling. So much misery and pain. The sky was a funny color, a sort of orangey-gray. Her gut tightened with nausea.

"Keep an eye out," Mei murmured before she moved to the rift and began to work the magic to close it.

"Don't suppose the irony of having a rift open at a place called Hell's Gate is lost on the Dark Fae," Card grumbled as he stood, eyes flicking from place to place on the horizon. "This place is wrong."

"It is. But it needs to stand. For remembrance," Ashe said quietly. "It's surprising to me that I hadn't thought of a place like this before as a magnet for dark magics."

They all spoke in hushed voices as Mei worked. It took her longer than any of the other rifts had before and when she finally got it closed and opened her eyes it was full dark.

"Are you all right? You were out for quite some time.." Concern etched Jayce's face as he ran fingertips over the nape of her neck.

"The energy here gave the rift power. It wasn't that complete a rift even, but it was difficult to envision it whole. To envision anything whole. Let's go, we have one more here on Earth and then we need to go to Sh'har."

"And we break for a meal after the last Earth one, before Sh'har. I brought the tea." One of Card's eyebrows rose, daring her to argue, so she just sighed and nodded.

The next rift spot was near Wounded Knee. The trauma was older than that of Auschwitz but at the same time it felt ingrained into the hills. There was magic there though, not just the smudge of darker magics used to open the rift but white magic, earth magic, healing magic.

"I can feel it, it's in the ground. Use it to amplify your own magic, Mei," Ashe said as he knelt with her. "Sometimes the kind of minerals in the land hold the event, the good and the bad."

Mei closed her eyes and reached for the positive magic and joined it with her own and it was easier to close that rift than the other one even though it took her nearly an hour.

Card helped her to stand and kissed her temple. "Now, time for a meal and a bit of a rest before we head to Sh'har."

They shimmered to Mei and Card's home in San Francisco. Mei took a nap while Card and Kai barbecued chicken and salmon. After some sleep, a good meal and some tea they headed off to Sh'har where, thankfully, it was full daylight and their risk was far lower.

"What is this place, Mei?" Rasa asked as he prowled around the perimeter of the spelled space.

"This is an execution dump for the bloodworkers," Bedwin snarled. "They bring their human blood slaves here when they are too old or if they *misbehave*.." Bed went off on a muttered rant but as long as she kept watch Mei was fine with that. She knew Bed had a reason to hate her own people even if she didn't know the whole story.

That rift took longer than the first one. Mei had a hard time visualizing anything hale and whole in that place with the stench of death in the air so strongly. She continued to dig deep within herself, throwing out all she could to try to heal the tear.

"She's having a hard time of it," Jayce said quietly to Card.

"Yes. It's this place. This place smells a lot like Carthau. The death and blood on every surface." Card shuddered. "I'm not even sure if she's realized it yet. I'd like to get her the hell out of here before she does."

"I'd like to get her the hell out of here before they find us. It's well after dark now. They've begun to feed. I can feel them out and about." Bedwin came to stand with them.

"Have you ever battled Sh'hari before?" Rasa asked, his voice a little louder than it had been before.

"Keep it down. And no. Mei killed them, I cleaned them up." Card's smile was feral.

"Well here's your chance," Rasa called. "They're coming and they know we're here."

They turned to see a group approaching. Sh'hari, Dark Fae and demon too.

"Pull her out of that, Ashe. We'll need her if we mean to stay and fight," Jayce said.

"We have to see if we can't grab one of these bastards. If it looks like it's bad we'll sift out. Try to take a Fae, kill the rest," Card said, hearing Mei's voice in the background as she came out of the magic she'd been working.

Instantly she was up and at their side. "Watch the magic. Demon magic stings like a motherfucker," she said as she pulled both guns out and aimed, taking down two of the Sh'hari before they'd even realized what was going on.

"Stupid. One of these days people are really going to start using guns," Mei muttered and they fanned out.

Ashe threw up a protective spell around them, one that would repel most of the magic thrown at them, but it couldn't stop the fireballs the demons threw. Luckily Bedwin and Card caught them and sent them back as Mei continued to shoot and duck, shoot and move.

By the time the two groups came together there were only five left, two Dark Fae, two demons and one Sh'hari.

Make that four as Bedwin reached out with lightning speed and snapped the neck of the nearest Sh'hari.

"Nice one, Bed," Kai roared as the battleaxe came down.

"Ew." Mei winced at the stench of brimstone as the demon was injured. Quickly, she took out both kneecaps of the last standing Dark Fae and bent to grab him to sift out. Only to feel the heat and then ice of a sword point searing through her side.

Things slowed down as she turned, not letting go of the prisoner.. Card and Jayce felt her injury through the bond and both moved toward her. She pressed a hand over the wound and tried to concentrate her magic there but she'd used most of it on the rifts.

"Down!" Rasa yelled and a sharp clawed paw swept out above her head as she went to her knees. Card, fully transformed, bounded through the last demon and ripped it to shreds before they all moved back and sifted to Tir na nOg.

* * * * *

"Mei? Don't let go, angel," Card's voice was still low and growling as he adjusted back to a humanoid form.

Because of the security situation, they'd had to sift into the gardens. Card picked her up gently and moved into the palace as Jayce followed, shouting orders, dragging the prisoner behind him.

Aine rushed into the room as Card brought Mei in and laid her down on a couch. "The healers are coming. But here." She went to her knees and, with an agitated motion, Mei's shirt was gone, the angry, red and still bleeding wound exposed.

Card paced the carpet near the couch, keeping an eye on what Aine was doing. Jayce burst through the doors, his face a mask of angst. The two of them stood and watched Aine work her magic on Mei just as the healers arrived and took over.

"She's fine. I've put her into a deep sleep so her body can do the rest of the work. Why didn't she heal herself? It was a severe wound, yes, but nothing a Fae of her age and bloodline should have let go this far." One of the healers looked up at the gathered group.

"She's been closing rifts for two days straight. We got into another battle last night on Earth. The first rift today took her five hours to close. She napped but they came on us after she'd been working for a few hours on the last rift. Her magic and energy were sapped," Jayce explained. "After her time in Carthau she is tired easily and extreme use of magic will drain her. She has restoratives she uses. She did today, we made sure of it. But she was already at a low point." He waited until the healers left to give more detail, knowing Mei wouldn't want any more people than necessary to know all the specifics.

"She can't keep doing this then!" Aine stood. "Why did no one tell me of this? I sent her off to do this and no one saw fit to tell me my child had been so deeply injured she'd be severely drained by the very job I was sending her to?"

"Majesty, pardon my excessive bluntness here. By the way, I'm Ashe, a friend and fellow warrior of the Balance with Mei. Telling Mei she can't do something is silly. She can. She does and has every day for the last nearly two millennia. You didn't see her at first. She could barely stand for longer than a few minutes but damn if she couldn't take out bad guys like lightning. It's why she took up handguns to begin with. She couldn't use a sword like she'd been trained. They tore the tendons in her shoulders and biceps, you know. Over and over

174

with cold iron instruments. She can use knives and long blades and is excellent at hand-to-hand but she can't use a sword."

Aine pressed her fingers over her eyes. "Sweet goddess."

Card rubbed his temples. "I don't like it either, majesty. If it were up to me she'd stay at home and let me and Jayce take care of her because she's precious. But she has a need inside her. It's a gift, this sense of righteousness she has. If you were to take this away from her she would lose faith in herself and I worry what it would do to her in the long run."

"Card is right. I wish he wasn't. Goddess do I wish he wasn't. But he is. She is a warrior. Has been for as long as I've known her. And out there in the field she's amazing. The only reason the demon got to her was because he vaulted over Kai when he jumped to avoid that axe. He saw me and feinted. It wasn't even intentional on his part. He spun to turn and grabbed one of the felled Dark Fae's swords and when he turned, Mei stood and he sliced into her with his movement." Jayce brushed fingertips over Mei's shoulder before conjuring a light blanket to tuck around her.

"And still she held onto the prisoner." Card chuckled.

"She's always been tenacious. Even as a baby. Damn it." Aine sighed and sat on the floor in front of Mei's unconscious form. "Pardon my manners." She looked up at the others. "Please be welcome in my home. I'll have rooms and a meal prepared for all of you."

Ashe and the others bowed at her introduction. Jayce stepped out for a moment to relay those instructions to Aine's secretary before coming right back to Mei's side.

"Thank you, Jayce," Aine said tiredly. "Wait. Prisoner?"

Jayce nodded. "A Dark Fae. He's in a cell and the truthseeker was on the way to see him when I came back here."

"Well, let's hear what the traitor has to say, shall we?" Aine pushed the worry from her face and stood. "I want to be there when he talks."

"That can be arranged." Jayce looked around, torn.

"Go on, you're the queen's Left Hand. I'll stay here with Mei. Come back and tell us what you find." Card squeezed Jayce's shoulder. "No harm will come to her."

"We'll all be here in this room," Kai added.

Jayce nodded with relief and escorted the queen out.

* * * * *

"It's very difficult for you, but I appreciate your putting Mei first, Jayce. It means a lot to her and to me too," Aine spoke quietly as they headed to the holding cells.

"I hate it. It tears me apart but Card is right. She's got a calling. I can't stand in the way of that or I'd be killing a part of her. A part that she needs in order to keep believing in herself.."

Aine turned to him before the entered the long hallway where the holding cells were. "You know, I've loved you like my own child for as long as I've known you. I'm fortunate to have you as my son and Mei is fortunate to have you as her husband." She kissed both his cheeks. "Now let's find out what's going on, shall we?"

* * * * *

Mei awoke to find the room filled with people eating and talking in hushed tones. She sat up and felt a slight pull on her side and remembered the wound.

"Angel, you're awake." Card smiled and plumped up a pillow behind her back. "How are you feeling?"

"A bit sore. I guess since I'm alive you got me to a healer."

"Don't even joke," Aine said crossly. She handed Mei a cup of tea. "Drink this. Tila is here. She's taught me and my healers to make your tea so you'll always have some no matter what home you're at."

"*Mameri* is here? You all shouldn't have dragged her here. I'm fine for goodness' sake." She sipped the tea and began to feel better as it hit her system.

"Here's a little clue, missy! I'm your mother and I'll do whatever I need to. Tila agrees with me and as she's a queen in her own right and your mother too, we both plan to team up on you if and when we have to."

Tila came into view and kissed Mei's forehead. "I've enjoyed meeting your mother, Mei. Now that you're awake I'm going to head back. You rest and drink the tea."

"You didn't have to come. I'm all right, really. I know it's birthing time in Lycia and you're needed there."

Tila waved it away. "Stop it. I'm not the only midwife in Lycia. It's just been six hours. I love you, silly child. If I were injured would you come?"

"Well of course. I love you too. But..."

"No buts about it. Now take care of my son. I'll see you soon."

Standing straight again, she kissed Card and the others before waving and popping back to Lycia.

Mei smiled. "Okay. Fine. Now what did you learn from the prisoner? Anything good?"

"She's like a dog with a bone, that one." Ashe grinned and handed her a plate. "Here, you may as well eat while we listen."

Mei thanked him and began to eat slowly.

"How's your side?" Jayce sat next to her.

"Feels a bit tight but other than that it's okay. I tried to heal it, it just wasn't happening. I'm sorry to have made more trouble for you all."

"Mei, stop that. I hate when you do that! We all know why you were tired. So stop being apologetic about it." Card growled and Mei patted his hand.

"You're right. I won't say I'm sorry. I won't even apologize for apologizing." She grinned and Card leaned in to nip her chin.

"Okay, so the news is they're under the gun. They need to get the rifts working by the deadline because Lorcan is running scared from Xethan and the demons. They've been trying to open rifts for centuries and only this season could manage to do it with the aid of some pretty nasty dark magic.

"The trolls, despite the fact that there've been rifts to Aurelia, are not taking part and that's why they let the demons in to start with. They're losing support because the Dark Fae don't trust the demons and there's been no progress. So they've been going back to the rifts they've opened to see if they can't open those farther. They've given up on trying to open new ones at this late stage."

Mei looked at Jayce with raised brows. "Won't that be interesting then? To set them on each other. Do they know we've been closing the rifts?"

"Not yet. But I think one of the demons may have gotten away back in Sh'har. If that's so, they do now." Jayce didn't want to tell her but there was no avoiding it. She had to know. "I injured him severely but I don't know if he was dead when we sifted out."

"Which means we need to get back out there as soon as possible. I'm going to eat and drink the tea and we'll continue."

The sound of teeth grinding played through the room but no one argued except Aine. "I know it's useless but I'm going to say it anyway. Why don't you get some rest before you go out again?"

"What is the date on Earth?"

"Hold." Jayce sifted and returned some moments later. "August 5. And there's no way of knowing what it is even now. We can't wait."

"Okay. I did rest. The healer spelled me into a pretty deep sleep and I've had tea and some food. There are three more in other universes and then two more on Earth. Let's do those in the other universes and then get back to Earth."

Mei stood and they all stood with her. She looked down and realized she didn't have a shirt on and conjured something along with her weapons.

"Mother, I don't want you leaving the palace at all until this is over. Please, for me. The closer they get to August 22 the more desperate they'll be. I don't want you caught in the crossfire. And yes, I know you're old and the queen and all-powerful and stuff but come on, I'll feel a lot better if you just humor me."

Aine narrowed her eyes but shrugged. "All right. But I'll still do Audience and go about my life. It's important."

"And Con and I have stepped up her guard detail so she's well protected," Jayce assured Mei.

"All right. Let's go then."

The seven of them joined hands and sifted from the room.

* * * * *

"She closed the rift? On her own? Multiple rifts even? And you're telling me eight mature cacodemons, ten Fae and four Sh'hari couldn't stop six?" Xethan's voice was calm, too calm, and everyone in the room stayed as still as possible to avoid his notice.

"Sir, she had a handgun and..."

"So what? Lead can't hurt us. What's your excuse?"

"No. The bullets are special. We sent a Sh'hari back to the scene to check. They have a core of cold iron and silver. The one demon she shot with the gun died from his wounds. The Fae she shot died as well." The guard kept his eyes downcast.

Xethan took a sharp breath. "That takes some guts. Shooting silver ammunition with her half-breed lover in the

179

fray. Creative too. The Messenger is no doubt responsible for that development. Should have killed him long ago."

"Please! You can't kill Carl Donovan. He's like some kind of god or something. And you people have bungled up this whole thing. It's nearing the deadline and we're here. I hate it here. Earth is bad for my complexion and I blame you." Eire's voice was petulant.

Lorcan groaned but didn't put Eire behind his back or attempt to shield her. Xethan liked it when people learned and so he wouldn't kill him just yet.

"You are the most stupid woman I've ever met. Milkmaids who've been repeatedly dropped on their heads are more clever than you are. Killing you will be such a joy. But not now. I'll save it for when I've got the time. And since you morons won't have any of these rifts open by midsummer, I'll have loads of free time in September. In the meantime, The Messenger is not *some kind of god or something*. Fool. He *is* a god. Still, gods aren't invincible. He's got a weak spot, just not one that I've been able to exploit enough to kill him. But again, free after August 22."

"Why do you let him talk to me that way? I'm your queen!" Eire stomped her foot in frustration.

"Eire, please go. You're not being any help at all," Lorcan said wearily and she stomped out. He waited until she was gone before continuing. "Just try not to kill her until after we've taken over. A figurehead will be important at first."

"Do you actually believe you're going to take over?" Xethan watched him lazily.

"One way or another. If not this year then next. I've spent thousands of years of my life preparing to take Tir na nOg back. Another Earth year won't make a difference one way or the other."

"Our agreement was for this one cycle. I have no intention on being a part of this ill-conceived plan for a single day past what we agreed to. You've lost the trolls as well."

"And the Sh'hari. It was one thing when it would have been a secret attack but now the Fae queen knows and I'm sure her Right Hand has informed the witches in New Orleans. I don't want a quagmire. I wanted a nice, bloody war that was winnable on surprise. You don't have that," Hamil, the Sh'hari leader, said. "If you can't make this work by the deadline, you're on your own." He turned and left.

"Sometimes desperation breeds creativity. You know they'll be looking to close the rifts that remain." It wasn't so much that Xethan cared about the Dark Fae or their cause, he wanted one thing and one thing only. Lorcan and his ridiculous vendetta was a vehicle for that.

"She closed the most important ones. The rift in Germany and the one in Sh'har. It's too late to try to use one in another universe. We need to stay here on Earth to watch the time. Oh! We should ambush them!"

Xethan sighed in disgust. "No. I swear you're as thick as your queen. I begin to understand why you've been at this thousands of years. You're not very bright. Now, what I think is that you should concentrate on getting a rift here on Earth opened before they get back here. If I were them I'd close the ones elsewhere to get back to Earth and close those last. Concentrate on the one weapon you may have against them. The rifts. Time here passes differently than in other universes. If you're lucky they may not even get back here in time and you can open it and bring the hordes through. Once it's open here you can press through the veil on their end in their universes. It's a very dim hope but it's all you have." Xethan stood and headed for the door, Mei on his mind. If and when she came back he'd be waiting for her, and this time he'd have her.

Chapter Ten

🔊

The next three rifts took a lot of effort. Not as much as the earlier ones but by the time they got back to Earth it was August eighteenth.

"I'm going to send Ashe to look at the other rift sites. Just to ascertain if he can feel anything unusual. When he comes back we'll check in to a very nice hotel near whatever rift site we decide is next." Card nodded and Ashe nodded once before disappearing.

Mei looked at Card, her eyes looking huge against pale skin. She'd done all three rifts in a row with not much time to rest. It had felt so urgent they'd pushed through.

He reached out and drew the pad of his thumb over her bottom lip, loving the way she sighed happily at his touch. "We'll get you resting soon, angel. You need a good meal and a decent eight hours' sleep."

They waited on some benches in a beautiful waterfront park for about twenty minutes before Ashe came back.

"One of them is nothing. No one here, just a slight bit of matter leaking. The other is a hive of activity. They're trying to work on that one. I could feel the matter from where I watched away from the group. Someone is giving them decent advice. They've stayed here and worked while we were elsewhere."

"Where?"

"Cambodia. The Killing Fields. It's not a nice place. It's also August in Cambodia. Even Cade is going to think it's hot."

"Let's close the other one. If we can't get to it before the deadline it'll leak matter until next year. And then we'll go to

Cambodia." Mei's heart quickened. This was nearly over. One way or the other it would end.

Jayce sighed. "All right. Let's rest for eight hours and then we'll go and close the rift. That'll also give us time to get some more troops to help. We're going to have a fight on our hands when we storm that last rift. Which means I want you, Mei, to have eight solid hours of rest in between the two rift closings. You're the only one of us with the magic to do it and you're running on empty."

"Let's go now to the next rift. Yes, I'm tired but if it's done we can rest. Ashe said there was no one there. Card, you can go and bring back some of your pack and Jayce, go and get as many Fae as you can without endangering my mother and the palace, if we fail, they'll need the backup. I promise I'll rest once we close the next rift."

"She's not going to give in," Card said with a sigh. "Let's go. I'll run to Lycia first. Then Jayce, you go to Tir na nOg and then Rasa, you go to the Donovan and get us some more warriors. We need as big an army as we can to get Mei to the rift. She'll need safety while she closes it."

"Okay, let's shimmer now and I'll get started. We're wasting time."

They shimmered to the spot in Siberia and Mei got to work while Card sifted out. He returned shortly with thirty-five Weres. They had their own rules about how many of them could be in other universes at one time and he also wanted to leave enough back at home to mobilize in case of full-out war. They immediately took up guard positions. Jayce touched his lips to his fingertips but Mei was deep into the spell, she didn't notice and he sifted.

As he returned with thirty-five of his men and women, Mei stood leaning in Card's arms.

"Cripes! You look knackered." Jayce rushed to her.

"I am. I admit it, I need to rest. Let's go." Her words were slurred, her eyes glassy.

Their small army shimmered away from the spot and into a very nice hotel in Hong Kong. First cloaked but slowly fully materializing to remain unnoticed.

"It's near but not so near they can feel us," Card explained.

Within minutes keycards were distributed and people ensconced in rooms. It was midday and everyone agreed to meet up in eight hours. Sentries were set near the rift site to watch for any activity that appeared to indicate the rift was opening.

Mei barely choked down her tea and fell asleep on the couch in their room. Card moved her to the bed, removed her clothes, lit some herbs in a brazier and set some white noise before returning to the sitting area where Jayce was just getting off a phone call.

Card collapsed into a chair with a long sigh.

"How is she?" Jayce asked. "She looked pretty damned bad earlier."

"When she admits she needs to rest it's bad. She's running on empty and needs the rest. Between four rifts and the sword wound, I'm inclined to let her go longer than eight if we can be assured there's nothing pressing at the rift."

"Let's monitor it and see. She'll be pissed off if we let her go too much longer, though. I hate this but I'm glad it's nearly over one way or the other. They're ready for war back in Tir na nOg in case we fail."

"Who were you talking to?" Card nodded toward the phone.

"Con. Because I wanted to leave a goodly number of Favored and other soldiers back in Tir na nOg just in case, I thought we could use some backup that didn't strain the number of off-universe visitors. A friend of mine, Con's brother-in-law, has a crew of some pretty tough people. Hunters. Con is shimmering them here along with a few Charvezes. Em is off somewhere safe with Elise. But many of the other witches will come to help. Rasa came by and told me the Donovan sent twenty-five of his warriors. Most of them skilled with battle but several mages and witches too. Earth is full between our people and theirs. No more sifting from offworld unless they can get that rift open."

"Ah good. Ashe said he counted seventy-five at the site, all Fae. But it was full day so most likely any Sh'hari and demons would have been in shelter from the sun. The demons can be out in the daytime of course but they prefer not to. And the Sh'hari can be out if they absolutely have to but their magic is severely muted because it goes to protecting them from the sun. I'd add at least forty more. Odds are nearly even but your friends from New Orleans should put us over the top." Card picked up the room service menu.

"Hungry?"

"Starving. I should have made her eat but I didn't want to wake her once she'd finally gotten to sleep. Do you need to rest?"

"I'm a seven-thousand-year-old Fae warrior. I need about two hours' rest every two days even though I do like my sleep. That's why it concerned me so much that Mei needed to rest so much more often. I hate that he's taken so much from her." Jayce's voice lowered into a snarl.

"I don't need much sleep either. I take it because I like the routine, like being with her while we sleep. But I'm fifty thousand years old. I'm good to go. Shall we eat and do some strategizing?"

"Fifty thousand? You're joking."

"Glad that facial cream is working so well." Card chuckled. "Demons have very long life spans, as do Weres. My father is seventy thousand and he's only now considered a Lycian male in his prime."

Shaking his head, Jayce conjured up a huge spread. "Let's eat and plan this. I mean to kill Xethan and end that threat to our woman as soon as possible."

Grinning, Card tossed the menu aside and they got to work.

* * * * *

Mei woke up and stared at the clock on the bedside table. It was eight in the evening and she'd slept a good six hours. Her magic rushed through her like electricity. It was back. Relief rushed through her as it always did when she felt her magic's return. Smiling, she got out of bed and stumbled toward the bathroom, where she took a very long, hot shower.

"Hey, angel. How are you?" Card hugged her, pressing a kiss to the top of her head when she came out to the sitting room. "You could have taken another two hours. You need it."

"I didn't try to wake up. I just did. My magic is back, I feel energized. I'm good to go." She waved at the table, where papers lay strewn about. "I see you two have been busy little worker warriors."

Jayce looked up at her, loving the sight of her face, the familiar curve of her smile. Desire slammed into him and both Mei and Card turned to look at him.

"Well hello there, warrior." Mei moved to him, straddling his lap as she sat and kissed him softly. "Got something else besides strategy on your mind?"

Card chuckled behind her.

"You feeling up to it? I know you're...shit!" Jayce gasped when her hand found its way into his pants, grabbing his cock and squeezing just right.

"Does that answer your question?"

He took her to the plush carpet then and she laughed, looking up into his eyes with total trust and openness. "Only with you, Mei. No one else can make me feel this."

"Fuck me. I need to feel you inside me," Mei murmured.

He thought their clothes away and lay skin to skin with her a moment until she opened her thighs, bringing the head of his cock to the entrance to her body. Quickly he rolled, bringing her atop him.

"Nice moves." Mei winked.

Card moved around and knelt behind Mei, kissing her neck, and when she reached back to guide Jayce, Card took over, grasping Jayce's cock and holding it as Mei moved back on him, taking him deep into her body.

She arched, her back curving her body into a beautiful shape, head back, hair trailing down her back, over his thighs. He looked up at her, breasts offered so temptingly he had no choice but to test their weight in his hands, his thumbs riding idly over her nipples. With each pass he felt her pussy contract around his cock.

Card grabbed her hair, holding her head as he devoured her mouth. His other hand slid down her shoulder and over Jayce's, their united fingers working her nipple.

Jayce loved the way it felt there, the three of them united. He and Card working together for her pleasure. Her cunt squeezed and released around his cock, juicy and hot. He felt the play of her inner thigh muscles against his hips as she rose and fell on him.

"So beautiful. Sexy. Everything right in the world," Card said, his lips skimming the column of her throat.

A burst of love so intense it burned the back of Jayce's eyes pulsed through him. He saw Mei through Card's eyes and realized she completed him in a way Jayce hadn't seen before. It was a gift of sorts, this perception through Card's emotions, and he realized not for the first time just how strong she was. She was more than her years at Carthau, her time in the field, her magic, her body and her beauty. She made his heart beat and Card's too.

That bloom of love and understanding pulled him under as he thrust up into her hard and came, her name on his lips. If he didn't draw another breath after that day, he'd have lived a life worth having. Because of her.

Mei found herself on her stomach, bent forward over a chair, Card's cock replacing Jayce's.

She loved being taken this way but right after Jayce had come inside her, right after she'd seen the depth of love and devotion in his eyes, it drove her insane with need. It seemed inexplicably hot to be fucked by one man moments after another, their bodies, sweat, seed, moans and sighs all mixed into a heady brew.

Jayce moved to the chair and sat, toying with her nipples while Card fucked into her body in short, hard digs.

"More," she gasped out and he hitched her hips up, widening her so he could take her deeper.

"Find her clit, Jayce. I want to feel her come around my cock," Card whispered hoarsely.

"Mmm, good idea. Is she slick for you then? Wet from me?"

Card and Jayce spoke around her and she shivered as four hands tugged, pulled, flicked and kneaded her erogenous zones.

She grabbed Jayce's cock and it pulsed back to life in her hand.

Her orgasm stole closer, gathering in her teeth, in the tips of her fingers, electric and sweet and she willed it, letting it manifest and settle into her until it exploded with a burst of pleasure so deep she couldn't do much more than just let it happen. She was theirs as they were hers. When she stood before that rift, whether they won or were lost on the field, her life was right and she was unafraid.

Card looked down at the feminine curve of her back, at her royal mark and the fingerprints on her hips Jayce had left, already beginning to fade. The wet sounds of their lovemaking sounded through the room. Every few moments the tip of Jayce's fingers brushed against his cock as he attended to Mei's clit. Each touch sent a shock of the forbidden through him.

He'd had her to himself for nearly two millennia. The idea of sharing her with someone she loved, who loved her as much as Jayce did, would have driven him crazy with fear a month prior but now as he saw the way Jayce watched her, the way Jayce touched her, it felt natural, right. Their lives had expanded to make room for another but it didn't feel so much like getting a smaller part of Mei, but rather their entire relationship had gotten larger and more complex. Change was often difficult, but this change, whether due to the various bonding spells or not, was right for all three of them. They were stronger for it, better. There was more love, not less.

He wouldn't be long. He often found it hard to resist Mei in that position. At that point her pussy began to flutter and then grip him, a gasp tore from her, low and deep. He ground his teeth and held back so she could get the most of her climax but no sooner than she'd relaxed he blew deep into her, bending and taking the tendons at her shoulder between his teeth with a growl.

"I love you," each one of them said softly, chuckling at the unanimity of the statement.

Chapter Eleven

Two hours later the group stood in a field two miles from the rift. The stench of dark magic laced the air, even from that far away. Jayce stood forward to address them all.

"This is it. Their last chance, the last hours to open the rift and if they do it, we're going to have to deal with tens of thousands of enemy soldiers here, totally beyond the ken and ability of the humans to deal with. We can't allow it. We are bound by covenant to protect them. We are bound by what is right and just to end this threat once and for all.

"Mei needs access to the rift to close it. She has to be close enough to work on it. She also has to be able to do it safely. Card, Conchobar and Rasa are on her guard. Ashe, Alex Carter and Lee Charvez will be the mages to protect her. The rest of us will fan out and take the offense until we can clear a path to the rift point. Once Mei is there it is our job to take out as many of them as we can. Do not waste any mercy but a quick death, they will show you none."

Card came then. "We begin the first strike with crossbows and magic."

Kael Gardener's hunter crew stepped forward with fierce-looking bows. "Thanks to Mei and the Donovan's people, we've tipped the arrows with cold iron. Very handy that," Kael, a wiry, platinum blond with tattoos and all manner of piercings, addressed them.

Card turned to Mei and held her face between his hands. "I love you. I will protect you to my last breath. You need not fear anything."

Touched, Mei leaned in and kissed him softly, tasting him, his love and magic on his lips. "I never worry with you at my back. I love you too. Don't forget you and Jayce promised me a trip to Tahiti when this was all over."

Jayce laughed, kissing her. "You taste like Card. I like that," he murmured. "Be careful. Your job is to close that rift. We'll make sure you can do that. I love you and I'm going to fuck the hell out of you when this is over."

Mei grinned. "Oh. Well, good. I'll be looking forward to that. And I love you too. Let's make magic and kill stuff, shall we?"

"So sexy when you're bloodthirsty," Card said with a wink. "Okay, in behind me, Con and Rasa. You're the big weapon so I know I don't have to tell you to let us take the risks."

Quietly, the group of just over one hundred warriors, witches and mages headed to the site. They bypassed the magical traps and on Jayce's signal the archers went first, taking out the first group and sowing confusion while everyone else headed down into the area where the rift was located.

"Shit, they've almost got it working," Mei shouted to Card over the din.

"Let's get you there then."

Mei tucked in behind Card with the others around her. Card had gone totally feral, his hands shifted into sharp claws and his eyes glowing demon yellow. Con's sword cut a path through the attacking Dark Fae and Rasa's lightning-quick blades helped clear the way on the other side. Alex, Ashe and Lee used defensive magics to repel the balls of flame from the demons.

Within a few minutes they'd gotten Mei to the rift. She watched dispassionately as their warriors took out the Dark Fae who'd been working the spell. They were trying to bring hell to Earth and she felt no pity for them. It was them or all of humanity and she chose all of humanity.

Knowing Card and Jayce would protect her no matter what, and knowing she had the power to break any hold Xethan would have to try to prolong her life if he took her again, she closed her eyes and began to work to close the rift, pushing the rest of the field out of her consciousness.

* * * * *

Xethan felt her as she came onto the field. It was dark but he felt the light of her soul, the beauty of her essence, from the knot of people charging the rift space.

He'd been content to watch the Dark Fae fools try to open the rift, felt the matter begin to rush out of the space. But he knew they'd never do it in time. Lorcan and Rennie seemed content to simply try year after year, to put up a solid fight for what they perceived was theirs.

But Xethan knew that if they'd truly believed Tir na nOg was theirs they'd have tens of thousands of warriors charging over the face of the planet already. When you knew something was yours, you fought for it with all your might.

He stood and began to make his way down to the fighting. To claim what was his.

* * * * *

Jayce caught sight of Xethan as he wove his way through the battle toward Mei. He turned and met Card's gaze and knew that the other man had seen him as well. The threat to their woman would end that night.

They could face whatever evils the universes sent at her, but the threat Xethan posed could not continue to stand. He'd never rest until he had her again and as such, they'd never rest until Xethan breathed his last.

Jayce raised his sword high and called a battle cry as he waded through the fighting bodies, taking the enemy down as he went, his ultimate goal to get to Xethan.

* * * * *

Card nodded to Jayce and watched with grim satisfaction as he moved to head Xethan off. His attention turned to a group of Dark Fae screaming orders to their troops.

"If we take her, we have the means to open the rift!" Lorcan screamed. Hearing it, Card growled, his muscles jumping, burning in need to go and rip the head off anyone who'd threaten his mate that way.

"Take out the ones protecting her but don't harm the princess."

A wave of Dark Fae roiled toward them and Card felt the balls of electricity pass over his shoulder and toward their attackers. He quite admired the tiny redheaded witch and her wizard mate. Together with Ashe, they'd held off any advance quite handily as Rasa, Con and Card had physically knocked back anyone who managed to get close.

He'd caught sight of the hunters and their hard-core hand-to-hand skills. He understood they hunted oathbreaker vampires so he didn't doubt their courage or raw viciousness for a moment. Still, he made a mental note to talk with them about some cross-training with Carl's warriors.

Bedwin was a blur of twisted necks and shining metal blades as she moved through the fray. He'd seen a gash on her side but it didn't slow her down and he hoped she had the sense to get out of there and back to the Donovan if the wound was severe enough. He'd seen a few of their people go down, mainly at the hands of the demons and Sh'hari—the Dark Fae were soft and most were already down or dead.

Card felt Mei in his soul, nestled against his heart. Felt her heat as she worked to close the rift and then the burst of satisfied pride when she finished.

"Done!" She stood and turned, pale but with battle on her face as she pulled her sidearms out of their holsters and moved to Card. "Okay, I can help."

"You'll stay behind me. You can shoot from there if need be. You're drained, I can feel it," he yelled back. "Good job, angel."

The ground thinned as their people fell. Fewer than twenty of their people still stood, mostly demons as the Sh'hari had either transported out or Bed had taken down. The Dark Fae, nearly all of them were dead but Mei screamed angrily as she watched Lorcan and Rennie sift away.

"Cowards!"

"They are, but that's not our problem just now. I'm going to start some cleanup here," Card said and began his magic that would incinerate the bodies and leave no evidence.

Con moved up and took Card's post to protect Mei.

"Good job, sunshine. Don't pout now, Jayce and Card both would have my ass for not protecting you and then your mother would chew up whatever was left. I know you're strong enough but let's just be on the safe side, you've worked a lot of magic in the last weeks."

Mei gave a frustrated growl of her own and Card chuckled as he continued to work.

"Look! Jayce is fighting with Xethan!"

Card stopped what he was doing and began to head in that direction. Mei watched in awe as his demon nature took over and his body began to steam.

"You'll stay here, sunshine. I know you want to do the killing yourself, but don't even give him the satisfaction of seeing you close up again. Let Jayce and Card exorcise this demon from your life and their own." Con spoke over his shoulder to her and she knew he was right. She'd made her peace. Jayce and Card deserved to do this for her and make some peace for themselves too.

There were no other moving bodies in the field but their people and Xethan so Con moved a little closer, but Rasa stood next to him and Ashe moved to Con's other side. Mei had to be content to watch over Con's shoulder as Kai and many others moved to get her back. Bed took over for Card but kept an eye on Mei as well. No one was going to take her or harm her and while she appreciated their protection, she wanted to rush to her men. One look at the set of Con's jaw and she knew it wouldn't be happening until Xethan was dead.

At least they were now close enough to hear clearly.

* * * * *

Jayce was a blur of blade and blood until he stood face-to-face with the demon who'd tortured and raped his wife for a thousand years and still was set on trying to take her from him again.

"You shouldn't have gotten involved in all this, Xethan."

Xethan looked him up and down and sneered. "Or what? You'd shake your braids at me? You'll do my hair?"

Jayce moved to slice Xethan with his sword but the demon moved quicker than he'd anticipated.

"You can't have her. She's mine. Always has been, always will be," Jayce said as they began to circle each other.

Xethan chuckled. "Is that so? With the half-breed's cock inside her?"

"He's mine too. Jealous?"

Jayce heard Card's laugh in the background and knew his mate would give him the chance to kill Xethan without interference but no matter what, the demon would not be leaving that field alive.

"You heard me. You. Can't. Have. Her. You couldn't break her. She never wanted you and even when you brutalized her for a thousand years you still never had anything from her you didn't take by force."

Jayce used his magic to push back at Xethan and then followed up with a kick to the gut but again the demon moved just out of reach of the sword tip.

Luckily he'd been paying enough attention to block the ball of flame Xethan sent his way.

"She loves me," Jayce grunted as his blade finally made contact with the demon. His blade was legendary and magical. Forged by the gods and handed down to the Fae when they moved from Earth to Tir na nOg. Con's grandfather had been given one and Jayce's the other. It came down to Jayce a thousand years before when his father had died and it sliced through Xethan's armor-thick skin with a sizzle. "Blessed blade." His smile was more a feral show of teeth.

"How hard up does a demon have to be? To try to force a female to love him?" Card taunted. "You're a high-level demon without any pride."

Xethan sent a flaming sword toward Card but Card batted it away. Jayce realized all their taunts had knocked the demon off balance.

"End it now!" Mei shouted and Jayce agreed.

He saw when Xethan's attention turned to Mei and her voice and he shoved the sword up and into the demon's chest, piercing his heart in one hard move. Xethan's eyes never left Mei, even as his life flickered from them and he fell to the ground and slowly burned into dust.

Standing there, stunned, he felt first Card's hand on his shoulder and then heard Mei running to him. He turned and she launched herself at them both and the three enveloped each other into an embrace of lips and tears.

Chapter Twelve

Mei lazily rocked herself back and forth on the hammock, the sound of the ocean lulling her, the crisp scent of the water and sand cleaning out the insanity of the months before.

Her head turned toward the shore, she watched Card and Jayce as they stood in the surf and fished, laughing like best friends.

"I'm glad this worked out for the three of you."

Mei smiled. "Hello, Carl. How are you today?" She sat up and watched her boss, looking smart in a linen suit, take a seat across from her.

He conjured a fruity drink in a coconut and sat back. "Better now. I just wanted to check in and be sure you were recovering. You worked a fair bit of magic in a very short time. You and your men saved the universes, Mei. Ask it of me and if I can, it will be yours."

"I'd ask for my stamina back but I know it's not a possibility. I'd ask to be able to carry a child but I know I can't. And so I thank you for being a father to me and for making me as whole as you could. I realize it must have taken some extraordinary favors to involve one as old as The Bona Dea."

"Ah sweet Mei. A face like an angel but the soul of a warrior. I will give you three a nice vacation but things are still brewing elsewhere and since Lorcan and Rennie escaped, they'll continue to be a threat. There'll be plenty of work for you when you're ready to return." He stood and kissed her forehead. "Now I'm off to pay a visit to your mother." His smile was wicked and she rolled her eyes.

"Ew. She's here by the way. On the other side of the island. She tries to give us our privacy but we were separated a long time and we have dinner several nights a week and I see her just about daily. Con and Em are here with Elise and several other Charvezes and their assorted spouses. Ashe and Rasa are here as well, in the town, where they can charm the ladies more effectively."

"It's a whole supernatural island." Carl shook his head.

"I wanted a vacation, they all did too. Why don't you stay awhile? My mother is staying in a rather large plantation house and I'm sure her accommodations are big enough for you."

"You'd be okay with that?"

"Donovan…Carl, I don't like that you didn't tell me. But I do understand rules. I know you would have if you could. I forgive you that. We all have rules, I suppose. And you and Freya helped with that spell that made it possible for me to be with both the men I love so much." Mei shrugged.

"You're a good woman, Mei NiaAine. I'm off to surprise your mother with some chocolates then. I'll be seeing you soon. Don't let your aim get soft, you'll need it soon enough," he said before walking down the beach and toward the other side of the island.

Card and Jayce approached looking sunkissed and windswept and absolutely delicious. Suddenly her bathing suit was gone and she faced two very eager males with nothing but ravishment on their minds.

"Go on then, make it worth my while," she said with a grin right before Jayce scooped her up and carried her into the house with Card following close behind.

Also by Lauren Dane
ʚ

eBooks:

Ascension

Cascadia Wolves 1: Enforcer

Cascadia Wolves 2: Tri Mates

Fire and Rain

Fun in the Sun: Sudden Desire

Reluctant

Sword and Crown

Threat of Darkness

Witches Knot 1: Triad

Witches Knot 2: A Touch of Fae

Witches Knot 3: Vengeance Due

Witches Knot 4: Thrice United

Witches Knot 5: Celebration for the Dead

Print Books:

Ascension

Cascadia Wolves 1: Enforcer

Cascadia Wolves 2: Tri Mates

Crown and Blade *(anthology)*

Feral Fascination *(anthology)*

Fire and Rain

Sexy Summer Fun *(anthology)*

Witches Knot 1: Triad

Witches Knot 2: A Touch of Fae

Witches Knot 3: Vengeance Due
Witches Knot 4: Thrice United

About the Author

🙿

Lauren Dane has been writing stories since she was able to use a pencil, and before that she used to tell them to people. Of course, she still talks nonstop, and through wonderful fate and good fortune, she's now able to share what she writes with others. It's a wonderful life!

The basics: Lauren is a mom, a partner, a best friend and a daughter. Living in the rainy but beautiful Pacific Northwest, she spends her late evenings writing like a fiend when she finally wrestles all of her kids to bed.

🙿

The author welcomes comments from readers. You can find her website and email address on her author bio page at www.ellorascave.com.

Tell Us What You Think

We appreciate hearing reader opinions about our books. You can email us at Comments@EllorasCave.com.

Why an electronic book?

We live in the Information Age—an exciting time in the history of human civilization, in which technology rules supreme and continues to progress in leaps and bounds every minute of every day. For a multitude of reasons, more and more avid literary fans are opting to purchase e-books instead of paper books. The question from those not yet initiated into the world of electronic reading is simply: *Why?*

1. *Price.* An electronic title at Ellora's Cave Publishing runs anywhere from 40% to 75% less than the cover price of the exact same title in paperback format. Why? Basic mathematics and cost. It is less expensive to publish an e-book (no paper and printing, no warehousing and shipping) than it is to publish a paperback, so the savings are passed along to the consumer.

2. *Space.* Running out of room in your house for your books? That is one worry you will never have with electronic books. For a low one-time cost, you can purchase a handheld device specifically designed for e-reading. Many e-readers have large, convenient screens for viewing. Better yet, hundreds of titles can be stored within your new library—on a single microchip. There are a variety of e-readers from different manufacturers. You can also read e-books on your PC or laptop computer. (Please note that Ellora's Cave does not endorse any specific brands.

You can check our website at www.ellorascave.com for information we make available to new consumers.)

3. *Mobility.* Because your new e-library consists of only a microchip within a small, easily transportable e-reader, your entire cache of books can be taken with you wherever you go.

4. *Personal Viewing Preferences.* Are the words you are currently reading too small? Too large? Too... ANNOYING? Paperback books cannot be modified according to personal preferences, but e-books can.

5. *Instant Gratification.* Is it the middle of the night and all the bookstores near you are closed? Are you tired of waiting days, sometimes weeks, for bookstores to ship the novels you bought? Ellora's Cave Publishing sells instantaneous downloads twenty-four hours a day, seven days a week, every day of the year. Our webstore is never closed. Our e-book delivery system is 100% automated, meaning your order is filled as soon as you pay for it.

Those are a few of the top reasons why electronic books are replacing paperbacks for many avid readers.

As always, Ellora's Cave welcomes your questions and comments. We invite you to email us at Comments@ellorascave.com or write to us directly at Ellora's Cave Publishing Inc., 1056 Home Avenue, Akron, OH 44310-3502.

ELLORA'S CAVE

Romanticon

Annual convention
for women who
refuse to behave

www.JasmineJade.com/Romanticon
For additional info contact: conventions@ellorascave.com

Discover for yourself why readers can't get enough
of the multiple award-winning publisher

Ellora's Cave.

Whether you prefer e-books or paperbacks,

be sure to visit EC on the web at
www.ellorascave.com

for an erotic reading experience that will leave you
breathless.

CPSIA information can be obtained at www.ICGtesting.com
Printed in the USA
LVOW13s0906180813

348440LV00002B/194/P